THE GOSPEL OF ORLA

THE GOSPEL OF ORLA

a novel

Eoghan Walls

NEW YORK • OAKLAND

Seven Stories Press
140 Watts Street
New York, NY 10013
sevenstories.com

College professors and high school and middle school teachers may order free examination copies of Seven Stories Press titles. Visit https://www.sevenstories.com/pg/resources-academics or email academics@sevenstories.com.

Library of Congress Cataloging-in-Publication Data

Names: Walls, Eoghan, author.
Title: The gospel of Orla / Eoghan Walls.
Description: New York : Seven Stories Press, [2022]
Identifiers: LCCN 2022033733 | ISBN 9781644212820 (trade paperback) | ISBN 9781644212837 (ebook)
Subjects: LCGFT: Novels.
Classification: LCC PR6123.A455 G67 2022 | DDC 823/.92--dc23/eng/20220721
LC record available at https://lccn.loc.gov/2022033733

Printed in the United States of America

9 8 7 6 5 4 3 2 1

For Leonie

1

I am sad to go but it is time now and there is no point in hanging around any longer. I leave my phone under the pillow. I don't leave a note because that is just for suicides. I don't want to make them sadder than they will be anyway but I also don't want them coming for me straight away. Last time they got me at the station but at least I hadn't bought a ticket so they don't know where I was going so they won't know where I am headed now.

I don't need to creep out full ninja as I can hear Dad snoring but I go into his room anyway to see Lily. She is down and will sleep until about half five in the morning. They are both deep sleepers until she gets thirsty at half five and climbs out of the cot into his bed and rocks him by the nose and that wakes him even if he has been drinking.

I will miss her but I can't bring her and can't hug her in case she wakes so I look at her for like a minute and touch her foot. Then I close the door and head downstairs and check my bumbag and rucksack and zip them up and tie my fringe out of my face and breathe and unlatch the door and step outside.

My bike is against the wall.

I walk it out the gate careful not to clunk anything.

The gate is creaky and Annie Pomfret's dog barks but he barks all night anyway and nobody pays him any attention. But I get out and check my zips again and there is no one up or down the street so I hop on and cycle out past the traffic light onto the bridge and there's no one in the Arms this late and I get down to the canal path sure no one sees me.

Now it finally seems like it might really work and I am happy.

I have piles of food in my bag and drink too and they are heavy enough but not too heavy. I have three chicken wraps from Boots and a big bottle of Fanta and a six pack of Hula Hoops squashed down to let the air out and four Curly Wurlys and fifty-four quid in my bumbag which should be enough to get at least one takeaway a day for two days if I get starving but I probably won't.

The plan is I am going to cycle to Liverpool get the ferry to Belfast then on to Drumahoe to Sinead's house and leave all this crap behind. Sinead would not chuck me out I am her dead sister's daughter and anyway I was born in Ireland I am like a citizen so if they want to take me back let them try. And I am taking the canals because nobody will look for me there. I got a book *Traffic-Free Cycle Paths in the Northwest* and could name all the rivers and villages I will pass through with my eyes closed. I left my phone so they can't GPS me and if they see my bike is missing they will be, – She must be on the roads! which is bullshit because I will be on the canals. I have googled everything and deleted my history. By the time they have figured it out I will be halfway to Ireland.

The towpath is dark but I have Mum's good light and it's not raining. A clear clear night. Moths are buzzing around the bike light and the muddy path is dry. When I clear the trees and pass out of the village I am nearly laughing. I pick up steam and slow to go under the bridge and the moon is massive. Really bright and pretty reflected on the water. And I reckon that is why I do not see the man in the bushes until he is right on me and the bike crashes into him and I go spinning off the path and he grabs the bike and I am hanging on his arm. He is holding me by my bag and my bike is swinging over the canal.

– Please, he says.

And I let go and I am in the water and help bloody hell he is going to rape me and kill me. He is tall and bearded and stank but I am in the water and the bike is on me and my clothes are stuck to my bike. And I kick and swim but the canal is not that deep but I am scared. I scream and say, – We have a dog, and climb up to the rushes and run. My trainers are full of water and so are my jeans and I run until I am down in the fields near Cooper's Ridge. The path is straight I have nowhere to go and I can hardly breathe and my throat is sore and I am getting an attack. But I do not hear him so I stop and hold my knees and try to listen past my breath.

He was mad hairy I do not know why he would hide in the bushes.

If he was trying to murder someone why would he be in the countryside? That would be stupid you are unlikely to find anyone to murder at this time of night.

I am still scared and out of breath and freezing but I can see him in the moonlight back where I crashed into him. He seems to be sitting down and I try the counting thing to slow my breathing. Suddenly I think maybe he is not a murderer but instead I have hurt him and I could end up in prison.

I am too young for prison. Obviously.

Still though.

My bag came off in his hands.

I have no bike.

My breathing slows.

Not perfect.

But better.

I don't know what to do.

So I stand watching and he doesn't move and I reach into my bumbag and take out the Swiss Army knife and wish I had taken a bigger knife the kitchen one but God I did not think I would be using it. I take out the biggest blade and slowly walk back up the towpath.

– Hey, I say. – Hey you.

He is hunched on the canal bank squatting and I can see him and he is really wearing a blanket. I think he is just some homeless guy but homeless guys can be murderers too. The only light is moonlight but he has a beard mad hair and shiny eyes. Either he has opened my bag or it opened when he grabbed me but my food is all over the ground.

He is putting it back in.

I am still afraid but more angry now as that was my bloody food I bloody stole it. Why is he touching it and for that matter where is my bloody bike? In the water that's where. So I start shouting like, – Give me back my bag! and, – I have a knife, and then more like, – I am going to bloody stab you if you move if you even move! And he drops the food in the bag and steps back into the bushes and bows his head. He says sorry over and over and his voice is deep and foreign and I grab for the bag and get it. Then I run past jabbing the knife about madly until I am on the village side of him and I reckon he could not catch me if I ran home.

And I will run but I am wet and I had a plan. Now I have no bike and I am scared but first I want to say something. So I turn and say, – What's your name? What's your bloody name?

He is squatted on the mud and looks up at me and says, – Jesus.

– Jesus? Jesus bloody Jesus like the Jesus Jesus?

He nods.

– Well bloody Jesus Jesus you ruined my bike. You owe me a new bike you arse.

And he says, – Sorry sorry, but now I reckon my knife isn't that big so I pull my bag tight and walk off and I don't look back and I don't run but when I get to the bridge I start crying but there is no one behind me. There is only one thing I can do which is go home and try this another day but with no bike I will not be able to take the canals. And I feel the world go out of control again and have to control my breath. So I do control it and walk back into Glasson shaking with cold and everything is still spinning when I hide my wet clothes in a bag at the bottom of my bed and change into pyjamas and lie back and wait and wait for sleep.

2

I wake to Lily taking socks out of my bottom drawer and putting them on the bed. She is playing Pack-the-Bag. It is seven
thirty so she will have had her bottle and morning sleep
but not proper breakfast. I hear Dad stumbling and cursing
around the kitchen getting ready so he is not having a bad
morning. Lily hands me my socks with the carrots on them
and I say, – Tata.

– Tata Orla.

– Tata.

Dad will be making her porridge and I normally bring her
down but I am sore down one arm and both knees. I pull
back my sheets and see brown muddy crap on both legs and
all over the sheets and I know I have to get this sorted. So I
let Lily take my carrot socks and carry her past the stair gate
down to the hall and call, – Dad take Lily. I need a shower,
and head back to my room before he can shout back.

I am really tired.

My clothes are bagged up but covered in stuff that stinks
of duck crap and probably is. He will know if he looks at
them I fell in the water. But since Mum died I do my own

washing and I reckon I can get them done without him seeing.

No the real problem will be getting to the ferry with no arsing bike.

I check my bag.

The homeless guy only opened one wrap. Or maybe it bust in the fall. But I can't be sure he hasn't touched the others and the Hula Hoops will go stale and screw it I am dumping the lot. So I take out *Traffic-Free Cycle Paths in the Northwest* it is not even damp and put the food in my bedroom bin and pile all the clothes with my dirty washing in case the guy touched them too.

Fuck.

I mean I can get more food but it will take me longer now.

Even longer with no bike.

I hear Dad turn off the radio downstairs which means he is feeding Lily so I have a clean run at the washing machine. So I pull off my bedsheets too and stick them and washing and all in at sixty to get the mud off and head into the shower.

My leg is cut but the scab is dry and I am all bruised.

The shower feels lovely on my head.

I need to scrub at my legs and face to get the muck off. We still have some of Mum's back scrubbers so I fill one up with shampoo and press it on the skin to let the mud rinse off. It hurts when I press it but I don't care.

I could walk to Liverpool but actually I couldn't.

I could nick a bike at school. They are all always locked.

Taxis would be a hundred quid and that's a stupid idea.

Money. I'll get money.

Then I will get another plan.

So by the time I get to that I am brushing my teeth with Dad shouting at the bathroom door that the woman from the council will be all over us if we are late again so I rush out in a towel and get dressed and find my mobile and he is already tooting the horn outside. So I grab the binbag from my room and toss it in the wheelie-bin and chug apple juice from the carton and grab my schoolbag and an apple and slip in the front seat.

And he's like, – Is that all you're eating?

– Yes.

He looks at me and I wonder if I still have mud on my face but I am sure I checked. Some mornings if he has been drinking he barely sees the world but today he is on the ball and he turns off the engine and curses and runs inside. I look in the mirror and wave at Lily.

– I'm going to school Lily.

– School?

– Yes I'm going to school.

– School.

I wasn't meant to come back.

Then Dad is here and he opens my door and shoves in my puffy jacket and a Belvita bar and it is chocolate chips. I don't need the jacket as it is near summer but I do like the biscuit so I take them both. As we drive off he keeps glancing at me.

– You need to eat love.

I shrug and get out my phone. There are so many WhatsApps I haven't checked it all night.

– You do, he says. – If you don't we'll get in bother.

I say nothing. We have had this fight before. I know and he knows that if the woman from the council tries to take custody off him it will not be because of my eating or lateness but because they think he is an alco after Mum died but I don't think they will take me or Lily anyhow. Jamie says they don't split families if they can help it. But we both have said our bit before so I shrug and keep reading as he drives.

There are WhatsApps from Majella and Sinead about the barbeque at Isabella's and there are texts and WhatsApps from Suzie B and Michaela and what looks like half of the class about some concert that Suzie B was at with a massive car crash she nearly died in. Same old same old boring shit.

There is still no text from Jamie.

His mum must have him blocked.

I shouldn't even be here I should be halfway to Liverpool on my stupid bike and I want to scream but I can't show anything or the game will be up so I look in the back and watch Lily.

She is fine with Georgie Pig.

I am going to miss her when I go.

It will take longer now but I am going to bloody go.

When we get into school there are parents fighting for parking and we are not even the last in. I get out of the car and Dad says, – Orla.

– What?

His eyes are far older than they looked when I was young.

– I love you pet. Take care.

I slam the door and put my head against the rain and head in.

3

School is school. Smells of Axe and rain in the morning but by Break it smells of farts and crisps. Jamie is still on suspension so I don't have anyone to talk to apart from Zoe who buzzes around and asks me to go to stuff. Everyone was all so nicey nice after Mum died even Suzie B who is a two-face slag and Sophie and Stacey but they are actually alright and I have been invited to every birthday party in my form since – even Suzie B's which had only six – but I am sure that is their mums making them so who could be bothered going anyway.

Mostly they know I'm a mad dog and leave me alone.

Suits me just fine.

I mean it will obviously be better when Jamie is back.

First Form then Science then Break. I sit in the toilet at Break and eat the Belvita. Then RE then Music and we go on the organs which is alright then Lunch.

Apart from the organs I am just planning. I could go to Boots for provisions but with no bike it could be five days walking and I might get sick of the same wraps. But if I get some money it might be different. Say I walked to Morecambe at night and got the first train – the 5.58 – that would get me in to Liverpool the same morning. But I would need cash for the ticket and there is a chance Dad or the cops will ask at the stations as soon as they realise I am gone.

But they might not ask at Morecambe station.

And it would be faster.

When I was got in the train station in Lancaster it wasn't my phone but they would have got me with that eventually. They got me because the guy who sells tickets knows Dad. I saw him staring and he must have let the platform guy know because then he started asking questions like was I Brian McDevitt's daughter and how was my dad and where was I going that early and I was watching the platform clock tick down and I kept thinking the train was going to come but it didn't so I bottled it and hid in the toilets and they called Dad and he came to pick me up.

Jamie says I should not pass the ticket desks just sneak in the back keep my face covered but he has been caught three times with no ticket and just legs it at the station he does not give a shit about anything just does what he wants.

But they know me at Lancaster but they don't know me in Morecambe and it is only what a ten-mile walk which I reckon I could do in one night all I would need is more cash but actually less provisions so it balances out.

As long as that tramp isn't on the path again.

I mean I can bring the kitchen knife.

But so Morecambe it is.

So I need cash.

So come Lunch I slip out into the rain. Dad has lunch pre-paid so I can't take the cash but I have eaten the Belvita so I am not hungry. But there is no harm in getting a couple of chicken wraps just in case. So I am glad of my puffy jacket because it is the best if you are going lifting. So I follow the crowd heading to McDonald's and turn in as they pass Boots and everyone is getting out of the rain crowding around the meal deals and it is the easiest thing to just put three wraps in my hand then over to check out the make-up and sneak them one by one up my sleeve.

No one sees me.

I once got told by a substitute teacher I was good for nothing but I am good at this.

It is a buzz but it is more of a buzz with Jamie.

His mum won't even let me near his house now.

But whatever he is not here and I need cash so I need to find the next lift. Makeup and perfume are no good no one buys them since Michelle McLaverty got suspended for telling Mrs Lambert to fuck off after she was forced to wash her face. Sainsbury's has stuff people will buy but the guy stops me at the door. Same for Tesco's. Same for Claire's Accessories. CEX keeps their discs behind the counter. Most of the smaller shops either have stuff no one wants or assistants that follow you. But Chapel Street Newsagent is sometimes good.

Once Jamie managed to get in to the till as the old fella who runs it is either soft or deaf.

So I go in and the same story. Packed with kids from school and pensioners hiding from the rain. They are all around the front of the shop looking out the door like, – Jeepers I'm not going out in that. And so I hang in the back of the shop and the old man can't keep looking at all of us and he stays near the till and then a woman tries to buy something from the shelf behind him.

He does not spot me near the storeroom door.

I duck in grab the first thing off the counter and duck out.

Now I have a carton of ten packs of cigarettes that I can sell for at least two quid a pack in one sleeve and three wraps in the other and I am walking through the rain with my head down grinning to myself like mad.

4

So I should be still down from losing the bike but still I can't stop buzzing. I dump the fags and wraps in my bag in the hall and no one looks at me and then it's afternoon registration so it's, – Yessir Mrs Arbuckle I'm here! then English then Maths and whoopdedoo Simpson is off and it's a supply who just passes out worksheets and I am on my own but I don't care I have my stash and can get cash as soon as Jamie is back to help shift the fags.

Zoe is by my locker hanging round to chat and what the heck I talk to her. She's saying Suzie B thinks she's great but she's not and I am dreading the bus but I have my stash so I say, – With any luck it'll be her that dies in a crash at the next concert. Zoe laughs out her nose and I laugh too and she looks at me as if she is not sure I am joking and neither am I.

Zoe is not bad. I mean she is not like Jamie but I have known her since Brownies and she has kept in with that whole crowd. All girl guides now. But we chat and she says, – Mum is picking me up so do you want a lift, and I'm like, – It's better than the bus anyway, and so we head out the front and I am sitting on the wall. She talks about Stacey and Sophie and then she says, – We're going to the circus tomorrow night if you want to come.

And I'm like, – The actual circus? With clowns and lions?

And she's like, – Yes the actual actual circus.

And we are laughing and she is not as bad as I sometimes think. And I can't go for a few nights anyway as I need to sell the fags and check ferry times and bus times again. And the circus is dumb but why would I not go?

– Who is all going?

– Just Stacey and Sophie and me. And my mum who is literally obsessed with us getting pregnant.

I shrug. – I'll ask my dad.

Then her mum pulls up in their big fancy four-by-four and she's waving out the window and sees me and is all smiles and I throw in my bag and try to get in the back but there are two car seats and Zoe's mum's like, – Come up front with me Orla, and I nearly don't get in at all but I am not sure I will make the bus now so I do. And I want to just chat to Zoe but Zoe's mum is all, – How are you love? and, – How's your father keeping? and, – You're so brave a very strong girl. And I'm like, – Yeah, and, – Uh huh, and, – Nnnnh, but for some reason she can't see I just want her to shut up shut up shut up.

So by the time we are at the corner I'm, – I'll get out here thank you bye, and she has to slam the brakes because I have the door open and I hop down and run into the house.

When I bust in the back door I can tell Dad has been drinking because there are cans on the counter.

Only two empties.

He will not be bad yet.

So I head to my room and take off my puffy jacket and before I can check my phone there is a ring at the door.

I look out the window.

It is Zoe's mum but Zoe is in the car.

Zoe's mum has my bag in her hands.

I run downstairs and I am at the door and Dad has not stirred at all. And I open the door and I'm like, – Why do you have my bag?

She's, – Orla will you please get your father for me.

And I'm, – Yeah but give me my bag though.

– Yes I'll give you your bag but please get your father first.

– Give me my bag now, I say. – The bag is mine. You have no right to my schoolbag.

– Orla I only want what is best for you. Please please go and get your father for me.

She rings the bell again and I think she is going to push past me and I grab for my bag and it is already unzipped and I see she has found the fags. And I am staring at her and her face looks all concerned but I don't care it is my bag she has no right she is not my anything it is my bag. And I am pulling and she is pulling and she says, – Please, but I am just as strong as her and then Dad comes up from behind me and reaches past and puts his hand in the bag and takes out the cigarettes.

– Thanks Orla love you got me fags, he says.

I look at him and so does Zoe's mum.

He has Lily on his hip.

He does not smell too bad.

He puts Lily down and she hugs my leg.

– You're Zoe's mam aren't you, he says.

– Yes.

He takes the wrapper off the fags and opens them up.

Takes out a pack.

He is drunk every night and drunk to the point of crying every weekend but I have never seen him smoke.

– Sorry I thought, says Zoe's mum.

– Thought what?

She blinks.

– Did you send Orla to buy you cigarettes?

– I did, he says.

He takes one out of the pack and puts it behind his ear.

– You know it is illegal to buy cigarettes under sixteen, she says.

– You opened my bloody bag, I shout but Dad smiles and steps between us and asks her in for a cup of tea as I grab my bag and Lily and run upstairs while Dad holds my cigarettes and chats to Zoe's mum and she eventually goes away.

5

Lily is on the floor and she has pulled out all of my clothes from the bottom two drawers and now she's putting them back in again. That's Pack-the-Bag. Dad has a fresh washing done and my muddy clothes from last night are folded on my bed and they look okay although you can still smell mud if you put them up close. Lily keeps talking to me but I barely look at her.

I am not going to get a chance like that in a long time.

Twenty quid is what they could have got me. Twenty quid is not much I bet most guys in my class could get it easy but Dad says we hardly have a pot to piss in and is wise to me stealing from him and never leaves anything lying around. Anyways I wouldn't take it he is not even working and the child allowance all goes on Lily. There was some money from Mum but what didn't go on the funeral went into the university fund. The university fund. Which is a laugh.

But whichever way I cut it I am in trouble.

I think about eating a Boots wrap but he is cooking downstairs and it smells amazing. And I do not want to see him and listen to all his crap but Lily is done with Pack-the-Bag and is at the stair gate.

– Daddy, she says. – Orla. Downstairs now.

And he comes to the foot of the stairs holding a dishcloth and shouts up, – Dinner! So I lift Lily but she wants to go down on her bum so I walk behind her and think about just going back up but I am totally starving and the kitchen is just there.

Dad says nothing but gets Lily in her chair and puts a plate of potato waffles and onion rings and beans in front of me.

It smells amazing.

He's like, – Eat up so.

So I do.

And he gets Lily in her chair and feeds her and I wonder when he is going to start and I can't bear it so I say, – They weren't my fags.

He looks at me and gets up to the kettle and brings down a single packet. *Lambert and Butler.* There is a picture of a man with one leg and a stump. SMOKING HAS BEEN LINKED TO TYPE 2 DIABETES. He slides it over to me.

– The rest are in the toilet, he says. – I flushed them. But I tried out smoking at your age too. It's not legal and it's not good for you. But I don't mind if you try it.

I keep my head down and eat my food.

– Is Jamie still off? he asks.

This gets me.

– This has nothing to do with Jamie. Jamie never went near them. He is still off and I've not seen him for weeks and you can ask the bloody teachers if you don't believe me.

He nods his head. He is feeding Lily. She eats the potato waffles with her hands but he spoon-feeds the beans to her as he can't stand the mess. Like she was still a baby.

Dad tries again.

– I wish you would stop nicking Orla, he says. – You have to stop.

He pauses but keeps looking at me as he spoons beans.

– You know the woman from the council. You know she will keep asking questions at the monthly meetings. I can't just take the blame every day because you will get caught some –

Then I crack.

– What about you and your drinking? I say. – That was two empties on the counter or was it three? How much did that cost?

Lily goes quiet and watches us.

He's, – They're still from last night.

I am pretty sure he is lying but not 100 percent.

– I'll not drink tonight, he says. – I'll lay off it all week if you promise to come in to Claire with me. I will.

Claire is the psychologist. She is a waste of space.

– All she bloody does is ask bloody questions and I don't want to answer her bloody questions and there is no way I am going back to that and you can't –

– Stop pet. Breathe.

He sees I am getting the breathing thing again. He sees it and backs off. He passes me an inhaler but I smack it out of his hand and push the fags back across the table and sit there and breathe slowly and I can control this and I know I can control it and I do.

When I look up Lily is pulling out of her seat and my last waffle is too cold to eat. Dad lets Lily down and starts putting the dishes in the dishwasher.

– I am not going to drink any more this week, he says.

– I am not going back to Claire, I say. And I go to my room.

6

He bloody does drink though. I hide in my room the rest of the night and he knows better than to disturb me. Lily comes knocking but I put the music up loud so she holds her ears and leaves. I know she only wants to play but when does my turn come? I mean I have loads to google now. Bus timetables from Morecambe to Southport. Southport to Liverpool. Fares from Preston.

Twenty quid would have got me to Liverpool easy.

If Zoe's stupid bloody mum hadn't looked in my bag.

If that arsing tramp hadn't sunk my bike.

I open my window and get under the duvet and flip through my phone in the dark. Lily goes down about eight then Dad watches telly and later he listens at my door and then goes out the back garden. I watch him from the landing. Drinking a sneaky can. Taking the cigarettes out of his pocket. He lights one and starts coughing and takes two more puffs and then throws it across the grass. Then he sticks the packet in the wheeliebin and I duck before he sees me at the window.

He gets to do what he wants.

Lily gets to do what she wants.

My stomach hurts.

I eat half a chicken wrap to see if it makes me feel better.

It doesn't. I bin the rest.

Another hour and he is snoring in his room.

I can't settle.

I mean I could go to the Arms and just ask someone for money. One of these randomers who always say they are sorry for Mum. But that is stupid they will tell Dad.

I could ask Zoe for the money.

Zoe's mum follows her like a helicopter.

I can't nick it in school. It would be easy but not worth the risk. Karen Wiltshire nicked a tenner from Darren Klassen's bag two years back and was let off with a two-day suspension but she was known as Gypsy Karen ever after until someone posted a video of her mum at the foodbank and that was pretty much the end of her.

I could rob someone. Like a stranger. A dog walker on the towpath. Hide like the tramp in the bushes with my face covered. Not like actually stab anyone I'm not psycho just scream at them with a knife until they hand over their money.

– Hey dickhead give me your money yo.

I try it in front of the mirror but my little Swiss Army knife looks stupid. I sneak down get the big kitchen knife and try it again.

– Give me your fucking money you want stabbed?

Works better. I mean I am too small.

The blade flashes if I wave it.

– Cash me outside yeah you want some fucking cuts?

Hoody up works better.

It is 01.10 and suddenly Annie Pomfret's dog is barking like mad and I throw the knife across the bed and duck down. Somebody is rattling our gate. I crap myself utterly and nearly scream for Dad. His snoring doesn't change so I look out the window and oh God it is the tramp from last night.

He has my bike.

He opens the gate but keeps jerking to watch Pomfret's dog as he walks the bike up the drive.

He could kill us all.

I grab the knife. Back to the curtains.

He puts the bike against the wall.

Then he turns and walks out the drive.

I watch him pass around the corner until the dog stops barking. There are other lights in the street but no curtains open.

Who does he bloody think he is?

I chuck on my leggings pull up the hoody and creep past my dad's room and head downstairs. I am scared but more angry and the knife feels good in my hands. I ease the latch on the front door and then stop and look at the fucking calamity that is my bike.

It stinks.

Like proper stinks like crap.

But worse there's weeds all knotted around the chain and the pedal bit. I don't know whatever way that moron dragged it through the reeds but the gears look like a nest.

I try to turn the pedal with my hand.

It turns and stops.

I try harder.

Water squeezes out the grassy gears.

For all the good it would do it may as well be in the canal.

That fucking bastard.

So I put the bike against the wall and pick up the knife and I head out Belmont Close. And there he goes ahead of me along the path in and out of the streetlights wrapped in that stupid blanket as if he had not just wrecked my bike. He is not looking around just toots along like an idiot and how the fuck does he know where I live?

He'll have no money or he would be wearing like a coat or human clothes. And I am not going to stab him. I am not. But he cannot come round here like a fucking stalker to my house in the middle of the night and who knows what shit he might say?

I am just going to scare him so he doesn't come back.

But I bloody will scare him.

It is dark as he leaves the edge of the village. No one around. The moon is bright then covered then bright again.

He keeps walking.

I follow.

After the first bridge he stops.

I duck behind a tree.

He kneels down on the bank and I see him put his legs in the water and walk down into the reeds.

He is clearly mad.

He pushes around in the water.

He is carrying something.

He is carrying a dead duck.

He puts the duck on the bank and climbs out and puts it on his shoulders and heads up the lane. He does not stop again on the towpath and I sneak behind full ninja quiet as nothing there at all.

I think he is going to eat the duck.

I feel like puking.

We pass two bridges. There are some taller trees and the odd sheep. But no traffic this far up the towpath so no one will see me whatever I do. But I am having second thoughts now. Maybe the bike will be okay. Maybe I can tug the weed out what is the point in scaring a man who is going to eat a dead duck. But then he crosses the weir and goes through a fence and heads for a barn in a field.

I think it is Daly's Barn.

Yes it's Daly's Barn.

The whole place stinks of dung but that is the country-side. The barn is not done up like the ones closer to the road. We came here once before Mum died before cancer and me and Dad were climbing on an old broke tractor in the rusty shadows after a picnic and Mum was shouting, – Get down from there you'll die the pair of you, but laughing shouting no sadness in it. That day stank of daisies and also dung. But now it is dark and I can barely make out anything but the tramp bending down outside the barn to a pile of clothes.

No it is a pile of bags.

He throws the dead duck down and I see it is a pile of other dead ducks or at least animals I don't know and oh God he is psycho I am going to puke but I don't I hold my breath and I want to see but I am afraid.

He lowers the blanket off his shoulders and he is naked but for some kind of pants or is it shorts? His shoulders are skinny his back skinny and his hair all raggedy down it.

He kneels down and picks up a dead duck.

He bites his arm and raises the duck to his face.

And I think he is trying to strangle it but he isn't. He puts the duck's beak in his mouth and the duck shakes in his hands. Like mad flapping its wings. The dead duck. Then the duck honks and shakes more and flap flap flaps and he puts it down and I see it walk away from him and it is not bothered at all waddling off in the moonlight with one quiet little honk.

I have the knife tight to my leg.

It hurts but I can't stop watching.

Because it has to be a trick. Maybe the duck was stunned or hit by a canoe or a skimmed stone or a dog shook it and that was that a stunned duck and nothing more. But then he goes to the pile and lifts another animal smaller it is a crow. And he opens the beak in his hands and puts his long thin wrist to its beak and I see his blood shine in moonlight and the crow takes it in and bucks and fusses like an umbrella shaking rain off and stands in his hand and says, – Krah krah, and hops up the barn roof.

And then one by one he takes the animals out of the pile like Dad at the ironing. Each one the size of a wet jumper or a hat or a glove. And I watch him shake them out to let air in their holes and feed them the faint trickle of blood from his wrists. He takes frogs from the pile yes frogs and feeds them and they hop away into the grass. There is a fox that has a crater in its face I can see from here but he lowers his mouth and whispers and the fox licks at his wrist and is whole again and stands by the bushes and looks around twice sniffing the air and dashes off. And birds. Pheasants and crows and a swan. Small birds – I think a robin or swifts I don't know names – but they drink from his wrists in the dark and flicker like finger puppets as he blows them alive and sets them free so they fly around him until the air vibrates.

My mouth tastes of blood I have bitten my lip.

My leg is sore and I have cut myself.

I look up and he is looking right at me through a cloud of birds.

I walk slowly towards him and remember the knife and hold it up shaking as I get closer and stare into his dark shiny eyes.

– My child, he says. – My child.

There are birds all round. I hold an arm above my head.

– Who are you? I say.

He's, – I am Jesus.

– The bloody Jesus Jesus?

He grins and his arms widen like he was going to hug me. In a field of wild zombie birds.

– Yes I am the Christ. Of God's blood. The Jesus Jesus.

I wave the knife before him.

– Well fuck off and leave me alone so.

He reaches out a hand and I stab at him but miss. Then I turn and run and the birds are all around my head but I duck and nearly slip into the water but catch my feet and steady past the first bridge and I listen but I am alone and I get all the way home and I lie in my bed and I stare at the ceiling and I cannot sleep.

7

So maybe I drift off about four in the night. I keep looking at my clock and thinking about what I just saw. It is like I can't fit all the thoughts in my head. I close my eyes for like a second and suddenly it is bright and Dad is in front of me and he's like, – Get up now for Christ's sake. I am too tired to fight back so I chuck my clothes on and he gives me two yoghurt drinks and a Belvita and pushes me to the car with his hand on my shoulder and normally I'd be like, – Don't touch me freak, but I am still thinking of how the birds moved in the guy's hands.

Maybe he could do that to Mum.

It's Form then English then Break then RE and the whole time I am thinking of it. And in RE I lift a Bible and spend the whole class looking under the table but the words are so small it is really hard to stay awake. Then Dawkins calls out, – Orla! Orla McDevitt!

And I'm like, – What?

And he's, – See me after class!

And I don't really care I just try to sneak out with the rest as Dawkins never remembers but he does remember and calls me as the class empties and I am too slow to make the gap between Stacey and Abeer and I end up stood at his desk.

And I'm, – What?

And he's looking up and he has one grey hair growing out the end of his nose but he says, – How are you doing love?

And I'm like, – I'm not your love.

He's, – I know I know that sorry love I mean sorry.

And he's not shouting at me in the slightest but no one shouts at me now.

Then he's like, – Did you not get any sleep last night?

And I say it's none of his business and can I go now. And he sighs and nods but says, – You can keep the book love, and as I go I nearly turn to him but just head on to Music.

I have half an idea to go out and steal a spade over Lunch. I never go to B&Q and there is no way they will know me. But I reckon we have a spade in the shed and anyway how would I get it out of the shop it's not going to fit up the back of my jacket. You have to plan these things in advance. So instead I go to Lunch and it's cheese and chips which is alright and then Zoe comes over looking guilty and although I am busy in my head she can piss off but she sits with me anyway.

– My mum is such a bitch, she says.

I shrug into my chips.

– But she says she is so sorry and she did not know the fags were for your dad.

I shrug again. Doesn't matter anyway. It was my bag.

– Where's Stacey? I say.

Zoe eats with Stacey most days. I can see Stacey anyway over chatting to Sophie and I think Andy from 10B. Zoe looks back at them and then down at her dinner.

I know she wants to be over with them.

I don't care.

– No but listen Orla, says Zoe and she's talking fast, – Mum says would you please come to the circus with us tonight and we are all going and it is her treat. And she says she is so sorry about yesterday and I want you to come too. We've not seen you for ages and it will be dumb and funny and won't you please come?

She is looking at me.

We used to be friends.

– The actual actual circus? I say.

She smiles and then drops it and stares at me a little scared.

And I have better things to do more important things than this now Jesus exists and that changes everything and my whole plan needs rethinking and my head is really sore and sleepy and I don't care what Stacey thinks of me or Zoe or for that matter her bitch mum but I did used to like Zoe. And I am tired but I think what the hell.

What the hell.

– Yes, I say. – I'll come.

And she goes red and says she will be at mines at quarter to six and I feel my ears go red too and try to plan in my head while she talks but eventually Zoe is too much and I head off to the toilet and then it's Science then History then home on the bus.

8

So I get home and realise pretty soon there is no way I can go to the circus but then stupid Zoe's stupid mum gives Dad a call and he's like, – What's this about a circus? and, – That's great dove I'll get your leggings out of the washing.

And I'm like, – No I'm not going, and we have a fight and I get shouty and I call him an alco and scream, – I'm not going, about ten times from the landing.

But he keeps getting things together and chucks the leggings into my room and I have a strappy sequined top I haven't worn in ages and he comes in with his wallet and he says, – I can give you six quid for popcorn but that's all I have, and I'm like, – I'm not fucking going, but he pretends not to hear the fuck and leaves the money on my table and although I have no intention of going I try on the clothes anyway and the top looks alright but you can see the spots on my shoulders and my neck looks scrawny. I know I could use the six quid but I am not going out with those bitches I am not even like them and I lock the bathroom door and sit down and cry.

Dad is out the door with Lily howling in his arms and he's, – Zoe's mam's coming in five minutes, and then, – You have to eat something, and then, – Here try this on this was your mam's, and although I don't want to go I don't know what he's got so I creep outside and have a look.

He's left a bacon sandwich at the top of the stairs and one of Mum's shawls.

I take them both in to my room.

The bacon sandwich is alright.

The shawl covers my shoulders. I still have spots on my boobs but if I pull the shawl together no one can see them.

It is weird wearing something of hers.

Not too weird as I never saw her in this.

It kind of fits if I pull it down the back.

Then there is tooting outside and I can hear Zoe's mum at the door. I cannot bear them talking because they are probably talking about me but I look out and Zoe is stood waving out the car window both arms spread and I laugh. She has seen me now and Stacey and Sophie too so now I have no choice so I wash my face and run down ducking under Dad's arm and Lily grabs my leg and I bend down and kiss her and hand her to Dad and I am in the car.

The girls are all chatting about their phones and I keep mine in my pocket an old crappy iPhone 5S but they are showing photos and I just look at theirs. But then we drive and Zoe tells them all Laura Cunningham got a lovebite on her boob from Ben Sharpe in 11D and Zoe's mum screams, – Zoe! and we are all laughing and then we are at the circus.

I thought the circus was going to be crap. But it's alright.

There are loads of people and we have to park in a field and walk past lorries and caravans and there is an elephant in a cage and I get my money out but Zoe's mum is, – Put that away, and pays me in. And it's dark and breathless and we are looking up profiles of year elevens on the phone but then it starts and there is a Scottish ringmaster with a whip and electric music and fancy lights. And the first bit is Chinese acrobats jumping crazy high and over each other and upside-down splits and fair enough but big deal. Like where's the elephant? But no one is looking at me they are looking at the guys so it's alright.

Then there is the tightrope girl sparkly in her dress she looks lovely but it is just a girl walking and juggling on a rope. Stacey is whispering away to Zoe and I am on the other side but okay.

But then the clowns come out and I think it is going to be stupider and it is. But then they call a volunteer and I think, – What if it is me? and we all scream and I laugh. But it is someone from the first row and they stand her on a chair and throw red apples green apples and a knife around her and a big clown in the end takes a bite from every apple and pretends to be about to bite the knife but throws it on. And the girl keeps ducking but nothing hits her and the fat clown eats apple after apple and it is getting funnier as no one can take all those apples and he is going to vomit and I think it is real and so does Zoe and Stacey and then he does vomit but it is a blast of ticker tape!

A blast of ticker tape all over the girl!

And I am laughing and so are the others and I am glad I came to the circus with my friends. We are all watching now and yes it is stupid but ticker tape and the face of the girl. And she takes a bunch of flowers and she bows and we cheer and everyone cheers and I can't stop laughing. And then I think, – What if I can't stop laughing at all? And now Stacey looks at me sideways and Zoe's mum looks at me sideways and the claps die down and I am still laughing.

It is half cough half laugh half breathing thing.

I try to stop.

I can't stop.

They are looking at me.

I think of the saddest thing I can. I think of Mum dead. Dead in the ground her dead bones her eyes. I think of oesophageal cancer. The hole in her windpipe.

But I am still making fucking donkey noises and I want to say, – Stop looking at me it is just my breathing, but it comes out like honk and so I get up and Zoe whispers to her mum and I squeeze past and knock over a young girl's popcorn but I am getting out. I am in the aisle wheezing big honk breaths and trying to cover my mouth with the shawl to stop the noise. I run out into the dark between the caravans and there is washing and there are barrels and portacabins and I duck under a barrier and I find a clearing to still my breathing.

I shouldn't have come.

I am squawking.

I stick the shawl in my mouth my throat stop my stupid breath.

In front of me there is an elephant in a cage.

An elephant.

A real one. An elephant.

She is huge.

Slow my breath. Slow.

There is a bandage on her leg.

Her eyes are wrinkly.

I spit the shawl out.

I do not know anything about elephants.

Her bandage is soaked in blood.

I walk up and look in her eyes. She is old and battered and the saddest thing in the world. Her eyes nearly all wrinkles. I feel like crying but I don't. I just stare at her and try to stop wheezing and I put my hand into the cage.

Her skin feels old and wrinkly.

I wish I could climb into her cage.

His cage. Her cage. I don't know.

I look around.

Fantasmo. Big letters on the side. Fantasmo.

Could be either.

My breathing slows.

There's no one here. Not in this bit right now.

For the maddest moment I think about breaking his/her lock and getting in and climbing on his/her back.

Maybe two nights ago I would have tried it.

Get him/her out. See what happens.

I can't climb in there now.

Now I have to work out what to do with Jesus.

So I wait by Fantasmo sniffing the big hay-and-shit smell of his/her breath. And I know I should go back in and smile at the girls and say, – Sorry about all that I had to go to the toilet, but I can't bear it and I know they will find me eventually and they do. It is Stacey who runs up and gives me a hug and then calls Zoe's stupid mum and they make a fuss and say do I want to see the rest of the show and I say no and there is a whispered discussion as they pull me from the elephant and pretend not to be angry and drive me home like I am some kind of special case.

9

So we get home and I am straight into my room past Dad who is not drunk yet. And of course they whisper at the front door but I have my headphones on they can leave me alone. I know Zoe is alright but I don't trust Stacey not to be all over Instagram with photos of the circus freak. Not that I care anyway.

But there is nothing posted yet.

– Orla can I come in?

Dad.

– No.

Pause.

– Can I come in love?

– I'm in bed already.

And he's pottering and he's not had booze yet so there is no way I am getting out soon and next thing I know I must have slept in my clothes because it's morning.

It's Saturday.

Saturday we sleep in all but Lily who rattles the stair gate until one of us goes down and sticks on *Peppa Pig*. But now I am up even before her so I brush my teeth and stick on jimjams and back to bed.

Maybe no one will post anything. Not that it matters anyway.

They're all assholes.

But there's nothing up yet.

I drift off until Lily comes in and we snuggle for a bit and then I take her down to the living room. There are eight cans in the recycle bin. He'll not be down for a few more hours so.

So I get Lily toast and Marmite and cut it into cubes and stick on *Peppa Pig*. She's like, – Not that one the other one, and I get it right after a couple of goes.

When she is fully absorbed I head out to peek in the shed.

I've not been in here for ages.

No one comes in here.

Everything smells of wet cardboard. Dad's bike is missing its front wheel and covered in spiderwebs. The lawnmower is right at the entrance but I think it's broken. The paper on the floor is yellow and dark and there is a box of tiles splayed over the floor. It is hard to get past things. The CD player. Scooters.

But I do find a spade up the back. The handle green. The edges all rust. Heavy enough and I get a splinter in my knuckle pulling at it but it comes free the second time with a clatter.

I leave it behind the shed door and head back in to Lily.

Dad comes down before eleven and we do Saturday. I mean some Saturdays when Mum was dying me and Lily were dropped at Bob and Sue's to give Dad a break but all their boys do is *Fortnite* and that's off the cards these days as Bob and Sue are getting a divorce. And Dad used to drive me to Jamie's but his bitch mum told him to stop bringing me over. No Saturdays now it's just us so I take Lily to the park and Dad does a shop and cleans the house and makes a nice tea and later goes to the pub and comes home blotto to fall asleep crying on the sofa.

So we do that.

I mean Lily finds a butterfly hairband in the park and I say it is nice. She falls and hurts her hand but there is no mark. The house is spotless and I mess it up again making towers for Lily. Tea is homemade burgers and onion rings and Dad has got me the sweet chilli sauce. We watch *America's Got Talent*. Dad comes down smelling of aftershave. He tries making jokes. Saturday.

But before he goes I have a go at the bike. There are tangled weeds all wrapped in the chain and whatever way I tug them they get stuck deeper. So I try to hack them with a screwdriver but the blade is too big so I get out my Swiss Army knife and use the smallest blade and dig into the fibres. Cover them with bike oil to see if that works.

It just makes greeny-black gunk that oozes when I turn it.

– What you got there?

It's Dad behind me Lily on his hip.

– Got it stuck in some reeds.

I didn't even have time to think of a lie.

He bends down and sniffs it.

– I can power wash it over at Bob's if you like.

I can't stand him hovering behind me so I walk it round the front and try to cycle it the length of the cul-de-sac. But he bloody stands watching from the garden.

Doesn't matter anyway. The bike is not worth crap now.

I mean it goes. But it's stop-starty. Like mad stop-starty.

I won't get to Liverpool on a stop-starty bike.

Dad says again he might have a look at it but I chuck it on the grass and walk into the house and pick up my phone. I know he won't touch it with his clean jeans on. But he always feels guilty before he goes out so he lets me flick through Instagram and Snapchat while he gets Lily ready for bed.

And then of course of course it has happened.

Stacey has put a picture up. I knew she would.

Not of me honking.

Just one of her and Sophie and Zoe all outside her house.

– Best friends after a mad night at the circus, it says.

A mad night. Best friends.

As if I wasn't there at all.

Liked by Zoe.

Liked by Sophie.

And Andrew. And more and more.

And I don't care. She could have taken the photo when I was there but she decided to take it when I was gone. But I don't care.

Because soon all these assholes can eat my dust.

Dad reads Lily her books and puts her down and then gets on his coat and comes in to me with a full pack of Prawn and Cocktail Pringles. – Here pet, he says. – Do you want to choose a movie off Amazon?

And I'm like, – I don't care.

He's, – Go on. Just choose one.

I'm, – Any I don't care, and he sits down across from me.

– Do you want to talk about last night? he says.

I roll my eyes and grunt. He tries to sit between me and

the telly and I move and he moves in front of me trying to be funny.

– Stop it, I say.

– Zoe's mum says you ran off. Said you got upset about the clowns?

I don't like Dad going to the pub. I don't like him leaving me with Lily as anything could happen what kind of man leaves a girl with her sister? I really don't like him pretending to be fatherly with his let's-have-father-daughter-conversations when I know he will come home blotto and crying and once he even came home bleeding. And if I did that they would take me away but it is okay for him is it? And I really don't want to talk about Zoe's mum and I don't want to talk about anything right now.

– *Captain Marvel*, I say. – I want to watch *Captain Marvel*.

– Oh, he says and gets it up on the clicker and puts it on. And then he goes around looking for keys and wallet.

– You sure you'll be grand?

– Yes.

He gives me a hug all stubble against my face.

– And you don't want to talk about anything?

– No.

– I love you pet. I hope you're okay.

He goes to the door.

– Call me if Lily wakes yeah?

And then he is out and I watch him go and I know I have a couple of hours.

I mean I cannot leave Lily and head out to Daly's Barn.

But I can dig up the cat.

10

I keep the back door open in case Lily wakes and drag the spade from the shed to the root of Sneaky's tree.

We planted the tree two years ago no two and a half when Lily was in Mum's belly and we had a cat called Sneaky because she was black except for one white foot and Dad used to call her a ninja with a sock. And clearly she was a ninja as she was out hunting one night and some woman ran her over and phoned the number on her collar and left a message where to find the body. As far as I could see the woman was a murderer. But Mum stayed talking me down off the walls while Dad drove out and I was sure it was the saddest thing that would ever happen to me. Then Dad came back with a plum sapling and the body wrapped in a towel and dug a hole in the garden and we had a cat funeral and read cat poems and went inside for tomato soup and rice crispy cakes.

So at least it will be easy to find her under the tree.

It is really hard digging up a grave. The grass is hard to get through and I have to push the spade into the ground with my shoulder and then jump on the blade and I keep falling and the tree is still small enough I could break it if I landed on it. But then when I get through the grass I have to peel it back like carpet and only then does the actual digging start.

It gets really sore.

On my hands and tiring too.

I could easily just give up but I have to see what happens.

There is so much crap in the soil. Big stones I have to lever out and broken pots and roots of the tree. I cut and tear at them with the spade. Saw them with the Swiss Army knife saw blade. Eventually I am covered in mud but I get on my knees and push my fingers through the soil until I think I feel the cat's towel on my fingertips.

I push my hands around the edges. I keep imagining maggots or slugs. For a second I sniff a sharp milky stink through the mud then I stop breathing through my nose. I get my hands under it and pull it out soaking and covered in stones and it is softer than I like to think about.

I lay it on the grass.

This is part one of my master plan.

Then I go in and get a bag-for-life and traipse some mud into the carpet and curse but put the cat in the bag and pat down the earth around the tree and put the grass back in place and put the spade and the bag in the shed. Then I brush the worst off the carpet and put my clothes in the wash and head in to the shower.

I am scrubbing my fingers when Lily comes in crying.

– Where's Daddy? she says.

– Aw Lily did you wake up?

But she is up now and no talking will settle her so I stick on Dad's dressing gown and take her down to watch *Captain Marvel*. She sucks Pringles from my hands and the crying slows and then I bring her to bed. I lie with her not even checking my phone until I hear Dad stumbling into the living room and I can smell his chips.

Lily doesn't stir.

It takes him half an hour to be snoring in front of *Captain Marvel*.

I head into my bedroom. I put on my dark leggings knickers bra a vest top and a hoody. Trainers. I look in at Dad and steal a chip and pause the movie. His feet are on the sofa and he has left the back door open. Or was that me? I am not sure. But I grab the big knife again from the kitchen and then close the back door and take the bag from the shed and hang it over my grimy handlebars and cycle up to Daly's Barn on my crappy stop-starty pedals.

11

Daly's Barn is different from two nights ago. The air is thick with moths that flap in and out of my bike light. There are bunches of quiet ducks in the water and I cannot remember ever seeing ducks swim at night. There may be more bats in the air too but it is hard to tell.

I throw my bike down at the weir and cross the canal and cut through the hedge up towards the barn. It is worse here. The bushes rustle with birds as I come near. There are rabbits on the actual path.

From the doorway of the barn I see light inside. There are lots of birds inside on the rafters and at the back the man in the blanket. He is sitting on a red plastic chair and in his hand he has one of those solar-powered garden lights Sophie has. There is a table before him covered in plastic bags full of papers. He is bent over I think reading a book.

He does not turn when I come in but the birds flap around muttering.

I walk closer and put the knife before me.

– You, I say. – Hey you.

He turns. The light is behind him and I cannot see his face.

– You, I say again. – What did you do to the birds?

– Child, he says. – I gave them the secret of life.

I nod.

I walk slowly over to him and put Sneaky's bag halfway between us and walk back to the door holding the knife up hoping I don't trip on like a goose.

– You owe me, I say. – You stank up my bike. You owe me.

I think he nods. Then he gets up and picks up the bag and walks towards me. I back off out the door into the moonlight glancing down to make sure of my footing and he just follows me slowly out until I can see his face better.

He smiles at me. Big beardy face and shaggy hair.

He does not look like he will kill me.

He does look very dirty and raggedy in his blanket.

– Do it, I say. Keeping my distance.

So he sits on the ground cross-legged like a primary school kid. And he opens the bag and takes out Sneaky's towel. I stand close enough to watch but keep the knife between us. He looks up and says, – Do not be afraid, and then unpeels the towel.

The smell is awful.

I think Mum must be turning that way in the earth and then I stop that thought.

There is gunk that could be yellow and the body looks like an old wrung cloth but then I work out a head. Yes I can see where the car hit it.

Jesus lifts his wrist to his mouth and bites the skin like he was biting an apple and out trickles his dark blood. And then he smiles up at me and puts the wrist to the cat's mouth and I know it is not going to work. But he presses his wrist into it and I see its back twitch.

The fur inflates. There is still gunk on it but the dead raggedy look shimmers like the fur was standing on end. Like a Van de Graaff generator. Like the cat was shaking itself awake with a shudder. And then rising on the towel with yellow gunk on the side of her face arches Sneaky our black cat who was dead stretching her back and digging her claws into the blanket of a cross-legged man on the mud.

I walk backwards and I do trip up on what a rabbit and I fall back and my breathing is going nuts and I need air and the cat is there licking her fur and I don't know what it means and the cat comes to me and I don't want to touch her and she yawns and she has a white sock and it is really Sneaky and if I do not breathe I am going to die. So I close my eyes try to slow my breaths I count them and feel something's wet nose on my hand and I jerk.

Jesus is crouched beside me. He puts his hand out to the cat and she licks blood off the ends of his fingers.

– My child, he says and uncurls one hand to me. – You are sick. Let me heal you.

And I swear he is going to touch me.

My breath is raggedy but I crawl army style on the grass and get the knife and I hold it up and I say, – I swear if you touch me I will stab you.

He stays where he is.

I can't see his eyes.

I breathe and count. Breathe and count.

The cat climbs up in his lap. I watch him stroke her. Watch him help wipe gunk off her fur with the edge of his blanket.

I breathe and count.

Sneaky scratches the ground every time she licks her fur.

My breathing gets better.

She comes over to me and puts her head next to mine.

I scratch her head.

I have not done this for two years.

I stroke her and stroke her and want to cry but I don't.

Instead I stand up and look at Jesus. I take Sneaky in one arm and she curls on me like she used to. I am still holding the knife. Jesus looks younger and less fat than my dad and he is lanky and dark and in the moonlight I can't see if he has any grey in his raggedy hair.

– Why are you here? I say.

I think he smiles.

– I am here to fulfil the covenant.

I sniff.

– No. I mean why are you here? Here here in Glasson Dock. Why are you here?

Jesus looks around.

– This is where I am, he says.

I don't know what he means. I have not been to church since Dad called Father Michael an obsequious prick and I never understood the gobbledegook of Bible talk anyway. So I ask a better question.

– Can you do that? Can you do that to people?

Jesus looks at me.

He nods.

I blink twice. My breathing is under control.

– How long are you going to be here? I mean here here in Glasson Dock.

For a second he looks puzzled but then he says, – I will be here until I am ready.

– Does that mean a couple of days?

– It means until I am ready. Until it is time to move on.

I nod. – So like until next Saturday.

Jesus shrugs.

– Until I have learned enough to move on, he says.

– Does that mean a couple of days though?

Another pause.

– Yes.

I nod.

Sneaky nuzzles into me. It is irritating and lovely. I put her in my hoody and zip it up like I used to. Never mind the gunk. I am really tired and confused and not sure if my breathing will stay where it is and I think this is what being high must feel like. I want to cuddle up in bed with Sneaky. But I also have to get Jesus some proper clothes if I am going to do anything with him.

– Okay. I will be back tomorrow night.

Jesus nods. But as I head off to the weir he calls after me.

– Child, he says. – You cannot take the cat.

I turn around.

– Why not?

I clutch Sneaky closer to me.

– Because I am the way and the life.

– What?

He stands. Keeps his distance.

– The new life is with me or not at all. The animal must stay with me or pass into the light of my Father.

I don't get it.

– What?

– The cat must stay with me.

I get really really angry for a minute. Hold Sneaky to my throat and do not want to let her go. But I am in control I am in control. There is always a cost to everything. So even though I don't want to I unzip the cat and put her down with a last scratch for her gritty ears.

– My name isn't child, I say. – My name is Orla. When I come back I will bring new clothes.

12

That night I sleep weirdly long.

When I wake it is 12.30. The whole house has a breeze running through it and smells of garlic and tomatoes. Dad has a bolognaise on the go and Lily is outside feeding imaginary sand to Big Ted with a plastic rake. I sit out with her. The day is cloudy but warm and she feeds me imaginary sand too. I don't like the rake up in my face but I play along.

– Tata Lily.

– Very welcome Orla.

Eventually she sits beside me and folds her arms on her knees like me. I let her copy me for a while and then I hug her. She is small and heavy and bony and the smell of the bolognaise is in her hair. I carry her in and Dad has set up the kitchen table with a tablecloth and has given us all wineglasses into which he pours Ribena which he calls ladywine. He calls us ladies and pretends to be a butler and I know this game from when I was a kid and he even does the cheese on the small side of the grater.

The food is okay. He makes good bolognaise.

I spend the rest of the day quiet enough. Flicking through

WhatsApp or Snapchat just working things out in my head. I mean Dad takes Lily out on her bike. Later he asks me to wash her hair and she lets me lower her head and no shampoo gets in her eyes and it's the first time I've managed it and it is amazing. Dad smells of booze the whole day but it gets weaker as the day goes on and when he puts Lily down he falls asleep in bed beside her.

I could easily go out to Jesus but I don't.

I go to bed.

Thinking.

It is like this for a few days. I go to school. Do Maths English whatever. I don't do the homework but the teachers don't expect me to. But I don't skip class either. I help with the housework do a couple of washings and fill the drier. I chat to Zoe and she doesn't bring up the circus and neither do I. Dad keeps his drinking down to a few cans a night and doesn't stick on his music after midnight.

Tuesday after school I come home and he has my bike clean.

– What do you think of that eh?

He dings the bell. It is out back and I catch myself because it looks amaze. All the mud is gone and all the fibres from the gears. He has managed to proper get in to all the teeth and the chain and it could be new.

– Aye that was Bob's power cleaner and a bit of bleach. You had it proper minging what the hell were you at with it?

I shrug.

– Well there was all gunk in there but I got it out. Fwoosh. Just blasted it out.

He hangs around at my shoulder jigging Lily up and down.

– It was crazy satisfying.

I try the pedals first with my hand and then climb up and give it a go on the road. The scratch of the chain is totally gone.

He calls out at me as I zip around the cul-de-sac.

– That's better now isn't it?

I ignore him. He keeps smiling at me like he made the bike himself and what does he want an Oscar? But I dump it on the grass and head up to my room. I mean he did a good job. But he doesn't work and all he has to do is watch Lily all day.

But it would get me to Liverpool now I reckon.

But there is a lot more now to work out.

To plan.

The odd time I try the Bible at night when Dad has gone to bed. The whole thing reads like utter gobbledegook from the start so I try dipping in at random pages but that is no better. I know from school that there is the Old Testament and then the Gospels are the sequel with Jesus in them so I read the Jesus bits but they are weird. There is killing and words I don't get even with Siri and demons and lepers and it all feels very very irrelevant.

But mostly I am planning.

I mean I will still go to Ireland. That bit doesn't change.

Mum is buried in Drumahoe in the McGonagle plot just round the corner from Sinead's.

But now I need to work out how to bring Jesus too.

Which has loads of complications. More food. An extra ferry ticket. Money. An extra bike.

That's not easy.

But by Thursday I have helped Dad get to the bottom of

the washing pile. He has not got this far maybe ever and says he hates it because now he has to iron everything. And I laugh with him as he piles bedsheets and raggedy pyjamas and tablecloths on the sofa and I ignore the can of Stella hidden behind the clock as he irons in front of the telly.

Because now I have a small bag of man clothes for Jesus. Four T-shirts and four pairs of knickers and a pair of old jogging trainers and four pairs of socks and one of jeans and one shirt and one jumper. The jumper has a Christmas pudding on it and I think that is pretty funny. They are all clothes Dad has not seen for ages and he will not miss them and so I stick them in my year-six schoolbag and throw in one of his old ratty toothbrushes and a tube of toothpaste and the big torch and I get ready to sneak out in the night again.

13

When I get to Daly's Barn Jesus is sitting out front with piles of books and newspapers spread around him. It is cloudy and there's a breeze so he has stones on the pages so they don't blow away. Sneaky sees me as I cross the weir and leaps up into my arms at the hedge and I carry her through.

The gunk on her fur is gone.

She smells like a cat all hair and electricity.

Jesus looks bothered. He is holding a solar-powered lamp to the paper but the light is pretty faint.

– Hi, I say.

He looks up. Goes back to reading. I put Sneaky down and pull the big torch out of my bag and turn it on and Jesus jerks at the light and I pass it over to him. He takes it from my hands and his eyes are wide.

– Child, he says. – Where did you get this?

He shines it across the pages. Bends closer to read them.

– It's my dad's, I say as I kneel down.

There are mostly newspapers and magazines. *Daily Mail. Cosmopolitan. Sudoku Weekly.* Sneaky nuzzles into my hand and I scratch her chin.

– What are you looking for? I say.

He shines the torch from page to page squinting up close as he does so. Curling in on himself over his lap.

– Some information, he says.

– What?

He glances at me.

– Some sign of the best place to go.

– What do you mean the best place to go?

He sighs. He puts a stone on his page and faces me.

– I mean the best place to announce myself to the world. To reveal myself to man.

I nod.

– Would you not be better off getting an iPhone?

He squints at me. So I pull out my phone and show it to him. I don't have 4G here but it seems I can get 3G not loads but a bit. He puts down the torch and leans over to see the screen as I open the search engine and type in *where should jesus return to earth*. I get a bunch of hits. Of course Wikipedia but also some holy websites and I pass the phone to him.

Jesus makes a little sound in the back of his throat.

– What is this?

– It's a phone. An iPhone. An iPhone 5s.

I reach over and show him how to scroll. Tap on the top site. *The Second Coming*: www.daysofchrist.org. I show him and say, – Here is how you scroll down you do it like this.

Jesus makes another noise and reads.

He gets used to the scrolling pretty quick. I sit at the edge of his books watching his blue-lit face and stroke Sneaky.

– You want to be careful, I say. – The battery I mean. It will run out in no time.

He looks up at me.

– In the torch, I say. – The phone will be fine for like an hour but I need to take that home with me but I can charge it then. But I am leaving you the big torch but I don't have batteries for it so when they run out you are back to those crappy lamps.

He blinks at me.

– Batteries, I say. – I mean oh my God do you not know what batteries are?

He blinks again and puts the phone down. He picks up the torch and turns it on the side. He feels around its bottom then the back and then the handle and finds the switch and turns it off. We are in darkness for a second. Then he taps the phone and it gives a small light to his face.

– I do, he says. – Yes I know what batteries are.

– But not what phones are?

He holds up the phone and turns it slowly.

– Aren't phones stuck in walls?

I shake my head.

– They used to be, I say.

– No matter, he says.

His accent is weird could be Indian or Scottish I am not sure.

– Jesus where are you from?

– I am from Nazareth.

– And you know what phones are but think they should be stuck in walls?

– No. I.

There is a minute where we stare at each other with only rustling ducks around us. He keeps looking down at the phone and then back up again.

Then he says, – The. It is. I am from Nazareth and I do not know how I know about phones.

– Well, I say, – You will need more than phones if you are planning on coming back and being Jesus. You look like someone out of a zombie movie and you stink like an animal. I got you these.

I throw my bag over to him.

He pauses looking at me.

– I stink like an animal.

– Yes.

He blinks slowly and looks down at my bag and I don't know if he knows zips but he must because he pulls it open. He takes the clothes out one by one and the phone goes dark as he holds them up in the shadow.

That is when I remember I have no knife.

I am not very afraid I guess.

Jesus stands and examines the jeans and makes a pile of clothing and then he shakes off his ratty blanket and then I turn my head quickly so I don't see his penis I just curl in to Sneaky and in a moment he speaks again.

– Thank you child, he says. – I should not go around smelling like an animal.

I look up.

He is dressed and standing above me.

– Where did you get the clothes?

– Nicked them from my dad.

– Nicked?

– Yes. It means lifted. Stolen. I stole them.

– Yes. I know what nicked means.

He sits down across from me.

– Child you should not steal.

– My name is Orla.

– Yes.

– You keep calling me child. I told you my name is Orla.

– Orla, he says. – You should not steal.

– Yes but they were at the bottom of the washing and he will not notice they are gone.

– You should not steal.

I sniff and rub the end of my nose. I have had this conversation with many people.

– Well somebody needs to dress you because you dress like a moron. And to be honest you need a wash too because your body still stinks and it is horrible. I didn't have space in my bag but I will bring shampoo and soap tomorrow and you can wash yourself in the canal.

He puts his head down and sniffs deeply and I think he is going to lose it and go mad with me but then I reckon he is just smelling his own body. Then he looks up and nods.

– I could use some soap but please do not steal it.

I nod.

– I will bring it but first you have to answer my questions.

He pauses. Looks down at his papers around him. The phone.

Then he nods.

14

So I ask him questions and he tells me his story surrounded by soft quacking ducks and the rustle of I think a badger. Feathers drift through the air. Sneaky is cuddled up in my lap and I would feel colder without her. Every now and again Jesus or me flicks a hand down to the phone to give our faces light. And at first he tells me stuff you could read in books. Bethlehem. Pontius Pilate. But I am not stupid I was in what five nativity plays and we went to Mass a bunch of times before Mum died.

– No not that, I said. – I mean how did you get here like here here to Glasson Dock?

– Glasson Dock?

– Yes.

– I. I walked.

– You walked from the Bible and ended up here like a thousand years later so you are now what a thousand years old?

– No. I walked from the sea.

– Which sea?

– I. I am not sure.

– What?

– I have not found a map.

– Wait a second.

I lean over and open up Google Maps on the phone. Show him how to open it and zoom in and out and his eyes widen and he reaches over and starts scrolling up and down and then spins it around and it takes a while loading and then I am like screw this I am asking questions and I pull it back.

He looks annoyed.

I'm like, – So you came into the sea in like what a beam of light?

– No.

He says it all firm like a teacher but I don't know why he is being a dick because it is my phone and if he wants to use it he can bloody answer my questions. I cover the screen with my whole hand to show him that I can take it away.

He is still for a moment.

– I don't know how I got into the sea.

I scratch my nose.

– So what just Bethlehem then BAM in the sea?

– No. Not that.

– So like a time machine?

– Listen to me!

Voice raised.

We both glance down at the phone.

He speaks more softly.

– If you want to hear me you have to listen to me.

I nod.

He bows his head.

– I don't know everything. But I know I woke up in a box at the bottom of the sea. The only light was a soft blue light that poured through a crack in the side of the box.

I have to lean in to hear him.

– At first I was not sure what kind of being I was. Human. Algae. Angel. But eventually it occurred to me that I had thoughts. And that I could see. And I saw that I had limbs and that I could move them. And in the soft light I could make out shapes and I saw those shapes were people and I knew they were dead. And I realised then that I was a person. And that I was not dead.

– Dead bodies?

He looks up. Squints.

I pull an invisible zip across my lips.

He closes his eyes and goes on.

– Words and memories were passing but I could feel something. I could feel the sun above even though I could not see it. On high somewhere a light was burning. I knew I had to see that light.

He sounds like a young David Attenborough. But like foreign.

– So I lay among the dead and taught myself to move. It might have been weeks or months. As I learned the use of my neck and my arms some memories came back to me. Songs. Words. Tastes. And one day I worked out how to move it all together and I pulled away from the bodies and swam through the hole in the box into the ocean.

I want to interrupt him but I can't so I bite my tongue and poke the cat and she digs her claws into my leg.

– I swam up. The brightness above me was the light of day and when I saw that I remembered more. Heaven. Prayer. What it is like to breathe on land. And I knew that I had lain with dead people and that I had risen. I was the Christ.

He makes long whispery finger movements as he speaks.

– It was hard to swim with no air in my lungs. My clothes dragged me so I shook them off and pushed into the brightness above. But as I did I could feel my skin start to burn. The brightness burning my flesh. Grey bubbles popped off my arms. My skin flaked. My body scalded. The higher I swam the more my body singed until I realised if I stood in the sun I would rise like incense from a censer. So bright was my Father's love that it would take me back to him.

And I am listening I am this whole time. And he talks of how he swam down under the water again but I have loads of questions like you burned in the water? How can anything burn under water? But I bite my tongue again and again but then one just slips out.

– Did you see any seahorses?

He tilts his head.

– Did you see any seahorses?

– No, he says.

I bite my lip. Then go for it.

– What about underwater cities?

But no no underwater cities either.

But he did see forests of seaweed and canyons where turtles pecked starfish off the rocks. Felt the water squishing him on all sides. The weight of water on his stomach and eyes. Clouds of jellyfish rising and sinking.

– What else? Like whales?

– There were huge basking sharks, he says.

And I'm, – Didn't they like try to eat you?

– Basking sharks aren't real sharks. They are a kind of whale with mouths like ribcages and only eat plankton.

– What's plankton?

– Plankton is. It's like a mist of germs in the sea.

But he gets ratty. His voice I mean.

– Do you want me to tell you this?

I blink.

– Yes.

– I cannot unless you stop interrupting me.

My fingers twitch. But I nod.

So he tells me he could not find the box again and slept buried in the ocean bed when the day got brighter. And over weeks in the ocean he remembered more. Like speaking and batteries and phones stuck in walls. Then another question slips out.

– But why would God dump you in the sea?

Jesus scowls.

– It's. It's.

He pauses.

– My mortal flesh does not have room for the infinite mind of God. But I have faith in my Father's goodness. I have lain with the dead. I have risen again. I am the Son of God here to bring love again to the world.

I could say more. But my head keeps dipping and my fringe keeps getting in my eyes and I am getting tired. I hide a yawn picking feathers off my knee and he says something about the sea and then something else and then another thing and then I shake myself and he is talking about swimming onto land.

– People! Alive! A village at the top of a beach! And in the middle a drinking house. Bright faces. Happy laughing voices. I was overjoyed. The first faces I had seen in nearly two thousand years.

And I try to stop myself but I can't.
– Wait. You said you kicked off your clothes.
– What?
– You said you had no clothes. Were you naked?
He looks annoyed.
– Yes I was naked. I came bearing love. I –
– Naked?
– Yes.
Sneaky is fully asleep now. Her breath a soft engine.
If I laugh I will wake her up but I can grin.
Jesus doesn't grin back. More kind of squints.
– At first I saw kindness in their hearts. And yes a woman gave me a blanket and told me to cover myself. But then there was shouting and a gnashing of teeth. One of them hit me with a bottle. They asked where my boat was and called me an illegal immigrant and tried to hold me captive until the police came.
I stop grinning.
– The cops?
– Yes. The police. And it was not my time yet to be taken so I ran before the light of my Father filled the sky. I took the blanket they had given me into this new land and I have wandered these pathways ever since.

15

Part of me wants to ask more questions. But my eyes keep closing and the phone starts to run out of charge. When Jesus sees this he stops answering with more than single words.

I mean he wanted to google all night and now he can't.

So we make a deal.

The deal is I will come back every night with a fully charged phone. He gets ten minutes online or on Google Maps while I cuddle Sneaky and I have to stay quiet but after ten minutes I get one question. My phone only has about an hour-and-a-half charge for googling so it works out about ten questions a night.

I can work with that.

So I make it work. I go to school and come back on the bus or let Zoe's mum drive me on Tuesdays and Thursdays. Eat school dinners instead of lifting. I fall asleep sometimes in class but they never make a fuss.

I perk up a bit in RE. Not for abortion or funeral rites but the Bible bits. Jesus casting demons into pigs and the one where he turns water into wine. I laugh trying to imagine him zapping wine with his fingers and wondering if he could make Dr Pepper or whatever. Dawkins gives me a short grumpy smile.

I go up to him at the end of class.

– If he could do that why wasn't he like ending world hunger?

– What?

Dawkins is shocked to find me at his desk I reckon.

– I mean if Jesus can make wine why isn't he making booze all the time and selling it? To feed the starving? Or just like feeding the starving in the first place?

– He did once. The feeding of the five thousand.

I have heard of this.

– The what?

Dawkins sits back and gives me a look. He chews his lip and then he answers.

– Does your dad take you to church Orla?

I shrug and shake my head.

– Do you want to believe in God? he says.

I shrug again. His eyes are watery.

– Basically, he says, – it doesn't matter. Some people believe and it makes them feel better and that's alright. Some people don't. That's alright too. But either way don't expect any of it to make sense because there is no logic in it at all.

He looks like he wants to say more but I reckon that is me done with him. I can read the stories myself and I have a better line to the truth than him. To be honest I am buzzing I know more than Dawkins. But I don't go lifting I keep my head down and try to remember to ask Jesus about magic food that night.

I forget though. I have it going round my head but by the

time I get home Dad is sitting at the table and with his concerned father-daughter-talk look. Lily is having a nap on the
sofa holding the head of the hoover. I try to duck out of the
kitchen after grabbing a yoghurt drink but he stops me.

– Orla, he says.

I head on.

– Orla, he says again hand on my arm.

– What? I say.

– Sit down love.

I slump into the chair and fold my arms.

– What, I say.

He sighs and opens my yoghurt drink for me and turns his
chair so he is in front of me.

– How are you pet?

I can't be doing with his hassle but I am keeping my head
down so I shrug.

– Is school okay?

He starts all the questions. Boys. Periods. Mum being dead.
Yadda yadda yadda. Would I like to talk to Sue or Sinead or
what about Zoe's mum never mind the bag she only had my
best interests at heart. Jamie and when he is coming back to
school. The usual crap but I can't afford to start a fight now.
But then he says one thing that makes me sit up.

– Were you digging in the garden pet?

I shrug again but look up to see if he knows.

– In the garden around Sneaky's tree?

I feel my heart pop slightly.

– Why?

– Just. Me and Lily were out today. The soil was all dug up.
Which is bullshit. I put the grass back I did. There was

some soil left on the grass but not much. But I am cool cool I am being cool.

– A fox? I say.

He looks at me and nods.

– It could have been a fox alright, he says.

If he knew for sure he would just come right out and say it and I'd be off talking to Claire and drawing my feelings and I can't be arsed with that. But I play it cool and then I am off upstairs and no one knows anything.

But it bugs me. I can't get it out of my head and when he starts snoring I creep outside to check it out. There is a fair bit of mud around the tree and some lines in the soil where you can see the grass has been pressed down.

But he can't be sure or he would just say it.

So I keep my head down. And take my time planning. Bikes and money and ferry tickets. And when I get to thinking about Jesus raising Mum I get so dizzy I could puke so I have to cool it because you have to be cool cool to get away with anything around here.

16

Those are the days. The nights are different.

Dad has a routine and is usually asleep after four to six beers and sometimes vodka too. Lily has always been a good sleeper except for the month Mum died. So I wait for Dad to start snoring then get on my hoody and head up to Daly's Barn.

Jesus is always eager to get online. I normally let him have a go before the first question and he looks up and nods after ten minutes. He counts them on the screen and never cheats. While I am waiting I cuddle Sneaky and try to ignore the ducks or badgers in the shadows as they freak me out. I reckon more birds are flying away as the weeks pass. But there are still a few feathers fluttering in our blue circle of light around the phone.

My first question is the obvious one.

– What is heaven like?

– Heaven is pure joy singing in the house of my Father, he says.

It sounds like priest talk. Nice enough just being happy and nothing else but it also sounds boring.

– So happy all day all night?

– Yes, he says.

– And the next day?

– Well time doesn't really exist in heaven. It is more just one never-ending happiness.

– Like now and then now and then now again happy happy happy?

He flicks the phone. I can see his face is scrunched.

– Not really moments. More constant. It does not fade like moments can. Happiness without end in the pure presence of God. But that is more than one question, he says and lifts the phone.

I think about that while I tease Sneaky's ear with the tip of her tail. Jamie once told me that his brother used to do heroin and that is the worst worst drug and before he died he told Jamie that heroin was the purest happiness. He ended up a heroin overdose. I often think about that. Happiness but so much you die. I can't imagine the endless thing not being like a prison.

So next question, – So in heaven you can't see anyone else is that right?

– God is there with you.

– Yes but not God. That was not the question. I mean other people.

– You know they are with you, says Jesus. – They are part of the altogether that is happiness with God.

– But if you all feel the same how do you know you are you?

He is silent.

– I mean can you look behind you? Like one minute

singing and then the next you know others are there and then back to happiness?

– There are no minutes!

It is like talking in circles. Timeless joy without break. But I use up too many questions trying to work it out. Like if someone died years before you can they be beside you in heaven? If you die old are you old in heaven? He keeps saying timeless happiness beyond the body but I imagine it as kind of blue singing.

Really there are more important questions anyway. I shouldn't have wasted time on anything else.

– So have you actually brought people back with your blood?

He nods.

– I have brought many people back from the dead. Perhaps you have heard of Lazarus?

I have heard about him in school or mass I am near 100 percent.

– But he. Lazarus. Him. He was back in Bible times wasn't he?

– That is another question. Phone first.

So I wait.

– So him. Lazarus. Raising him. Was that now or was it back in Bible times?

– That was long ago. I haven't brought anyone back from the dead since I came out of the sea. But I have brought back all these animals including your cat. People are just a larger form of animal. Except for the soul of course.

I hand the phone over and sniff Sneaky's fur.

It goes on like this. And he tells me all kinds of stuff. His life too. Like about sleeping in the ditches. Like one night he pulled his blanket back to find a flock of sparrows had crept in and nested on his chest and picked at scabs from his wounds and flew off when he rose. Tells me he once pulled a drunk man from the canal who cursed at him and lumbered off. Says he watches the villages most nights from the shadows and sneaks in before sunrise to take books or papers from the bins.

But then other nights I push the bigger questions. Stuff I tried not to think about when Mum died but that sends Dad raving when he is drunk.

Like, – So if God is good then how come people die?

I reckon he's going to say life is a test or some crap about God being smarter than us and human meat is too dumb to get it.

But he's, – That is what life is. Life is growing and makes no sense without death. If there was a garden or a jungle that just grew and grew all the space would fill up and there would be no room for light or new plants or leaves. It is the same with the heart. Do you think people can just grow and have kids forever and fill the world with more people? Grandchildren upon grandchildren without coming to blows? Earth would be a spinning mess of confused never-ending families.

He reaches for the phone. I pull it back.

– Bullshit, I say.

His hand hovers in the air. He watches me.

– I told you heaven was eternal. To be eternal it is timeless. Because if you have time you need change and change is a manner of growth and growth without former states ending becomes so full and complex any non-infinite being cannot process it.

I blink.

– There is eternal life, he says. – That is what you get with my Father. The joy. The unchanging foreverness. You get that in heaven. But you also get the shortness of life here where love grows because it can change and can be lost. Tenderness and forgiveness are only possible because of suffering and the possibility of change.

I pull the phone closer into my hoody. Normally I don't play games with him but my throat hurts.

– Bullshit, I say again. – Why did Mum have to die?

There is silence in the grass. Sneaky jerks a little in my arms.

I cannot stand him saying this and if he tries his that-is-an-other-question bullshit I am walking right now.

He sighs.

– The dead stay on Earth in the holes they leave more than the holes they fill, he says. – And so the world fills with absence and pain but through pain we learn to comfort and pass into timeless –

– Bullshit bullshit fucking bullshit.

I growl. Zip up my hoody and push the cat off my knee.

He stops. Slumps a bit. Coughs.

– I do not have to come here, I say and I mean it.

He looks me in the eyes for a long time.

– I am really sorry she died Orla.

It takes me a while. I want to curse at him and run home. But actually I need him. So I hand it back and my next few questions steer clear of heavy topics. I ask about dinosaurs and love at first sight and the end of the world and whether aliens are real.

It goes on like this for weeks.

17

During this time Jamie comes back to school. I see him in assembly and get a mad buzz. I have got used to him not being around or answering my texts but finally he is back.

I mean he is not my boyfriend but me and him are mad dogs we do everything together. Lifting. Going round the caravans. They got him for a bag of iPhones in his locker but they have been after him ever since we shot up Lemons's car with an air rifle. But now he is back and it is on.

I have someone I can tell everything to.

Nobody even gives me a clue he is coming and he is clearly in a different class now because the first I see of him is in assembly. But no matter I head straight over grinning.

– Mothafucka, I say.

But something is wrong. He keeps his hands in his pockets.

– What's up?

He looks down.

– What's up? I say again.

– Go away, he says. – I am not talking to you.

– Fuck off. What's up? Was it bad?

He shakes his head then looks up.

He has shaved his moustache.

– No Orla, he says. – I am not allowed to talk to you.

I can't believe it and I feel rotten.

– Jamie, I say.

His face twists but he shakes his head.

– No Orla. I promised my ma I would stay away from you. I said I would and I will. So fuck off. Just fuck off alright. Fuck off.

He wipes the side of his nose with his thumb and dips his head away from me off in the direction of 9D.

And I want to call out but my guts feel torn so I just watch his back but then I see Carrie Oliver's classroom assistant looking at me whispering to Mr Dawkins so I go and hide in the toilets.

Jamie's mum can fucking go and die.

I feel all sick and shaky.

She thinks I should have taken some of the rap for shooting Lemons's car but I didn't hit it once Jamie was the crack shot. He got it every time. That wasn't even what they got him for anyway.

And maybe she is right. But she won't even let me phone him.

And now this.

I hide in the cubicle and miss Science for the first time in weeks.

I mean I don't give a shit. I have Zoe.

Screw Zoe though.

Screw Jamie too.

Screw Jamie more.

I want to puke.

But it doesn't matter. None of this matters.

I can just go.

I just have to get on with it.

So I need three things. A bike for Jesus. Food for two people for three days. And cash. Two singles on the ferry is fifty-eight quid plus some extra to get us from Belfast to Drumahoe.

I already have sixty quid in the bumbag so I need some more. The bike is a problem as the bikes here are always locked and the guy at Halfords knows me. But I can get food. So I skip out with the year elevens at lunch and follow them down the high street and nip into Boots. Three chicken wraps in my sleeve and I am out the door light as a slice of bread. But then I am like what?

Jesus can magic food out of nothing.

If he can bring a duck back to life a Zinger Tower burger should be like easy. And so food is no issue. I am making things more complicated than I need to.

And maybe his food will taste amazing.

So I can't take the wraps back but I take half a bite of one then bin the rest and head back for History and French then at home I barely touch my tea just thinking of magic food. Lily is down by eight thirty and Dad at quarter to eleven so when I head up Daly's Barn I am near cross-eyed with starvation. But I take Sneaky and give Jesus his minutes and when he looks up my mouth is watering and I'm, – So could you make me something to eat Jesus?

And he's, – Are you hungry?

– Yes.

He nods. It has taken to drizzling the last few nights so we sit in the barn. When he stands I notice again how tall and skinny he is. His jeans need a wash.

But I am watching his hands to see the magic. But instead of some kind of energy or biting his wrist he walks to the doorway and quacks faintly and picks up a duck. He lifts it and strokes its head and then puts his hands around its neck.

He twists and tugs.

Its neck snaps and it hangs like a bag.

And I am on my feet and I jump and push him shouting, – No, and I scream and then pull the duck out of his hands and it hangs still warm and I drop it and run to the other side of the barn. Breathing.

– Why did you do that? I say. There are tears. I am angry.

Jesus stands stuttering.

– I thought. I thought you wanted to eat together.

– Yes but. But –

– I can cook it if you like. Shall we light a fire?

I can't speak. I look down at the dead duck and the crowds of other birds milling around the door. I count my breaths and start again.

– Is this what you have been eating every night?

– Yes, he says. – I need to feed my body on this earth. Why did you think I raised them?

– I don't know! I say. – I didn't think about what you ate.

– It is okay, he says. – It is okay. I can make this right.

In the shadows I see him roll his sleeve up and bite his wrist and kneel down to the bird and he is going to feed it his blood and I shout again.

– No! Don't do that! Don't.

– Why not? he says on his knees.

I don't know why not.

But this is wrong.

– Just – just take the phone, I say and throw it at him.

He sits in the dark for a while.

I try not to look at the duck. It is just a heap on the floor.

– I am sorry if I upset you Orla, he says.

I look away.

He switches on the phone.

And he did upset me and I am not sure why. I was a vegetarian for two months when I was eleven but I gave up. But I know one thing and that is I cannot leave Sneaky in the barn anymore. So I control my breath and wait in the blue light of his googling and my next question is this.

– Do you still have the bag I gave you with the clothes? Your clothes need a wash.

And he leaves what he is wearing on him but gets a pile of manky T-shirts and sticks them in the schoolbag. And I start yawning and say I am going to head back and take the phone off him but when I get to the weir behind the hedge I crouch and call for Sneaky.

– Psss-wsss-wsss, I say. – Psss-wssss-wsss.

She comes padding through the long grass. Lifting her one white sock and three black feet over the stems and rubbing the side of her mouth against my hand. I am not sure how I will take her on the bike so I take Jesus's clothes out of the schoolbag and hide them under the hedge and there is room for a cat so I pour Sneaky in the bag pulling the zip over her head and put it on very gently and cycle home.

She only starts miaowing as I pull up the drive.

The lights are on in the kitchen but Dad is snoring upstairs.

When I unzip the bag Sneaky busts out. She scoots around the kitchen. Sniffing where her litter tray used to be. Rolls on the carpet. Scratches up the arm of the sofa.

Not much has changed in here since she was buried. All the baby stuff I guess. But we did not throw much out after Mum died.

Maybe the house smells different without her though.

I want to sit and watch Sneaky but I am actually tired and I need to hide her. The attic is no good and neither is the bag room as Dad is in the house all day. The shed would be alright as the grass in the back garden is too long to play in and the mower is broke but there is no way to stop Sneaky clawing her way out as the latch is crappy.

But I reckon I have seen the cat carrier in the bag room.

The bag room was supposed to be Lily's room but never got finished and now it is just full of bags. Mum's clothes and magazines and other stuff we haven't thrown out. Dad never goes in but Lily sometimes pushes through the bags. It was me who packed most of it as those were the days when Dad was a total good-for-nothing drunk loser but I think the cat carrier is under the coats and it is and I dig it out quietly enough.

Downstairs Sneaky is going proper mad. Hurtling around the living room and up the curtains. But there are five cans and a quarter bottle of vodka on the sideboard and hopefully Dad will sleep.

I try to get the cat in the box.

– Sneaky. Sneaky. Come on Sneaky.

She will not get in.

She is back in her kingdom.

We have no cat snacks now of course but there are a couple of leftover sausages in the fridge and I slice one up and get two saucers out and fill the other with milk.

Sneaky is very interested in the milk.

– Come on cat.

I put the saucers in the back of the carrier and she climbs in and I close it on her. And it is near impossible to carry a cat carrier with milk in it and not spill it all but I try hard pulling the light on in the shed and carry it awkwardly past the mower with two hands and when I look in Sneaky miaows but there is still milk in the saucer and I have done an amazing job.

I rub her nose through the bars.

Then I pick up the paddling pool and drape it over the carrier so you can't see her from the door. Then I pull off the light and stand in the garden and close the door and listen.

I can't hear her.

Then I go in and remember to get changed which is good because I fall dead asleep without even checking my phone.

18

Next day is Tuesday. Mrs Arbuckle corners me after registration. Stands at the door so I can't get past and touches my arm half pulling me to her table.

I don't know what she has on me but I can't think of anything.

– What is it Miss?

– I just want to chat to you Orla. That is all.

She always says my name like Or-lay like make-the-toast-or-lay-the-table. That usually bugs me but right now I am racking my brain to work out what she has on me.

– Is it the hoody Miss?

I tug my sleeves.

– Dad says he is getting the new blazer at the end of the month.

She keeps filling in a form on her desk but her mouth turns up at the edges.

– No Orla it is not the hoody although the sooner we have you in proper uniform the sooner we can get the year head off my back.

She clicks her pen and puts it down and looks up at me.

– No. It is just to be sure that your dad is coming in this Friday. We're supposed to do this once a month since Mum died.

– Just the counsellor thing is it?

She nods.

– Nothing out of the ordinary. But I thought I would ask if it has all been going okay?

I shrug. What does she want?

– It's fine.

She leans on her elbows.

– No problems in any of the classes?

– Why? Who's been saying anything?

– No Orla nobody's been saying anything.

She looks again at her notes.

– You are still not handing in homework for nearly anything and are falling asleep in class. However Mr Dawkins says you have been paying a lot more attention. And actually your attendance has improved quite a bit recently.

I don't think she has anything. I look at the clock.

– I'll be late for French Miss.

Mrs Arbuckle rubs her head. She reaches one hand out across the table but I pull back and her hand has to rest on the register.

– Orla we are not trying to catch you out. We just want to help. Give you a hand with anything that will help you get the education your mother would have wanted for you.

Bitch. I bite my lip. It is like she is trying to get a rise out of me and I will not give it to her. I pick up my bag and turn to the door.

But there is one thing. I stop and turn back to her.

– Why is Jamie moved to 9D?

She looks at me from the desk. Her face looks confused a second and then she straightens. Arranges papers on her desk and turns her body to me.

– Orla you know better than that. I am not allowed to discuss another student's private details with you.

We look at each other.

My face is saying fuck you.

She moves up beside me with a lowered voice.

– But I can tell you in any case when we move a student after a suspension it is normally in discussion with the student's parents.

– Mum.

– What?

– Not parents. His mum. His dad's left.

She stutters for a second.

– I can't –

But I turn off and head down the corridor. She is worth nothing at all. She calls something after me about counsellors but I have to consent to any further counselling outside the monthly arrangements unless they make it a required factor in a behavioural agreement so she can stick it up her hole.

The day passes. I am still angry by Tech. I'll have to go back to Boots now after binning the wraps yesterday but I can't risk it two days in a row so I try to chill over lunch with Zoe and Stacey and Sophie.

Sophie keeps denying she has a date with Andrew. They are all watching *Love Island* and agree Lara should be the winner. William Oakey is letting off a firecracker in the toilets after lunch.

No one is even talking about the circus anymore.

I think about the elephant in the cage. Fantasmo.

The saddest elephant in the world.

English then Maths then I climb in the back of Zoe's mum's four-by-four. She is happy enough talking to Zoe about piano exams but I hold my bag on my knee all the same. When she rolls in the dock I wave them off and turn and then stop.

Sue's car is outside the house.

Her boys aren't in the street.

I can't hear them in the garden either.

When I open the front door I call out. Lily is not there to greet me. The house is weirdly tidy. I hang up my hoody and there are no plastic bags on the hangers.

I look in the living room and there is nothing on the floor and the ironing has been folded in a pile on the armchair.

The place has been hoovered.

– Dad?

There are no beer cans anywhere. Normally if Sue was coming the place would be tidied a bit but there are no toys on the ground and the buggy is missing.

– Dad?

The kitchen is spotless. It smells of bleach and cigarettes. There are no beer cans in here either and the dishes are put away and Dad is sitting at the table. He has shaved and his face is red raw and I think he has been crying.

Out the window I can see the shed door is open.

I feel my breath going and I want to leg it but my legs are watery and my face goes cold. I can feel the breath sticking in my throat. Dad is looking down at the table. I can see the sun through the hair on the top of his head where he has started going bald. I let my bag slide to the floor.

He turns his face up to mine.

– Sit down Orla, he says.

19

This is what happened.

Normally Lily has playgroup on a Tuesday and Dad hangs around in his car outside while the mums drink tea but today that was cancelled because Jemima is having a baby and nobody could cover. So they came home and decided to play in the back garden instead of the front. They were going on a bear hunt so the long grass was perfect. They sat out for a while and then he came in to make pasta and fishfingers.

Lily was pulling at the shed door and Dad opened it for her. He looked in and saw the bikes and lawnmower but thought she would be okay if she didn't go in too far. He told her to be careful and went to turn the fishfingers.

Two minutes later he heard screaming. He thought she had caught herself on the lawnmower and he rushed out.

He found her screaming behind the door. At her feet there was the body of a cat burning on the grass. Smoke was pouring from the cat's body and it smelled like a barbeque and burnt hair at the same time.

He grabbed Lily and saw she was not on fire and took her inside but she would not stop screaming. He checked her belly arms and legs and only her fingers were red but it was hard to tell how bad. So he wrapped ice in a wet towel and told her to hold it tight. There was still a fire at the door of the shed so he put her down and threw the pasta on the fire but it was not enough so he tried to get the hose working and managed to attach the nozzle and sprayed the dead cat and the shed door where it had started to blacken. All the time Lily was crying and dripping water from the ice melting in her hands.

The fishfingers got burned too.

When the fire was out he went in and put Lily on the sofa before *Paw Patrol* and held her until she quietened and checked her fingers again. A couple of blisters but nothing terrible. Then he got her some bread and butter and sprinkled sugar on it and she ate it on the sofa.

When she was quiet he stepped over the charred remains of the dead cat and into the shed. He found the cat carrier and the dirty spade. He went to Sneaky's plum tree and dug up the grave and found it empty. Then he went in to the kitchen and threw up and threw up until he had nothing left to throw up.

His next move was to call Sue. They talked on the phone for about half an hour and she agreed to come over for a few days until he could sort something out.

Then he went to my room. He found my bumbag and the money but looked through everything to see if there were drugs. There were not. Then he cleaned the rest of the house. He put all the booze in the bin and scrubbed the floors until Sue came and took Lily who was now asleep out for a walk and then he kept cleaning until I arrived home.

He says all of this like he is apologising. He keeps staring at his hands and sometimes he whispers. In the middle I lose all control of my breath and try to count it out but I can't and he gets the inhaler and puts it on the table between us rather than handing it to me and I have to use it.

As he tells me he has gone through my things he takes the bumbag out of his pocket and puts it on the table between us as if I was free to take it. I want to grab it the money is mine but I cannot move. Then he unzips it and puts all the money in his wallet and lays the empty bumbag on the table.

As he nears the end the front door opens. Sue is getting the buggy in but her voice is hushed and then Lily tries to come in here but Sue grabs her into the front room and sticks on the telly.

At the end Dad says he has heard from some old boys at the Arms that I am always out cycling at night but he never made a fuss as he thought I was getting better. But now that has to end. I have to go to Claire and he has tried to pull it forward but she can only see him on Friday with the school thing so that will have to do.

He says he will do everything he can to make sure I can live with him and Lily but right now the most important thing is to get me the best care available.

His voice breaks a little as he says this.

Then he asks me if I want to say anything.

I stare at him.

My breathing is nearly normal now.

I could speak if I had something to say.

I have nothing to say.

He says he loves me and rubs his face. Then he makes an

odd gargling sound and looks down. He asks me if I wrapped the cat in petrol rags or what kind of fucking monstrosity did I come up with.

I have nothing to say.

He nods and holds his hands together. He says I will not be allowed to leave the house except for school. And Sue will be here to help watch me as he knows I can climb out the windows. Then he holds out his hand and says he needs my phone.

I say it is in my hoody in the hall.

– Just fucking get it then, he says.

So I am out in the hall. The door to the front room is open and I see Lily sitting down on the sofa and she waves at me and says, – Orla. Sue is sitting on the arm of the sofa with her legs crossed and she meets my eyes.

I look at the front door.

She has not locked it.

I look at Sue again. She is tapping her foot. Then her eyes grow wide and she lurches forward and says, – Oh don't you dare.

But it is too late I am out the door and on my bike whipping down the other side of the dock and in about thirty seconds I am over the Tide Path where cars cannot follow and they have no way of knowing if I am heading to Caton or Garstang or up the canals and by the time they check out one I could be as far as Lancaster or even halfway down the A6 to Preston.

20

So I head up Lancaster way to shake them off. If they see me near the towpaths the whole thing is blown. It is sunny as anything and the path is full of dogwalkers with sheep in the fields either side until I am in the city. Then there is a bit near the road where Dad or Sue could be waiting to get me but I head round the back of the train station then through the posh houses then back on the towpaths and I know my way to Daly's Barn from here.

I am starving. It must be about thirteen miles some of it mud paths and it takes me a few hours but I don't care I am too angry to eat.

I can't stand the idea of Lily hurt or the fact that Sneaky is dead again because of me and I can't stand the sight of my dad crying sober. And I can't just stop thinking about them because the way I stop thinking about stuff is making escape plans and right now my plans are not worth shit. Dad has my money clothes phone and everything. All I have is my school uniform and my bike.

If I go back to get anything they will get me.

But there is one thing I can do and that is go get Jesus.

So when I get to the barn there is a big pink sun starting to set and I cycle across the weir then wheel the bike by hand through the hedge.

There are no animals in the grass now.

I guess they hide in the barn with Jesus.

I guess if they go out into the sunlight they burn up.

Near the door I see small pile of feathers and a patch of ashes. Up close it looks charred and greasy. Maybe this is where Jesus plucks and cooks them. Or maybe one of his I don't know geese came out and burned on the grass.

There are bones in the ashes.

Inside Jesus is asleep in the furthest corner from the door.

There are crows roosting on his body.

The floor is rocks and birdshit. His chair and his books are piled in one corner under plastic bags.

I look through the piles until I find a stick.

It looks like the leg of a coffee table.

I push the crows off Jesus. They crow and hop gently aside. He is still wearing my dad's jumper and jeans both criss-crossed with creases and bird crap. His sleeping face makes him look like an angel with a big beard.

I have never gotten this close to him.

My own breathing is totally under control.

At first I am going to beat his face but I can't do it but I can beat his chest and I do. He jerks with the first whack and screams a second later and I get in a second whack before he can raise his hands. But then his eyes open and he covers his head with those long skinny arms but I don't care I beat his arms the crows squawking and flapping about me. I whack him and whack him and he screams and then stops screaming. He doesn't grab the stick but he winces every whack looking up through his arms and he looks sad.

The birds are mad and it is too frustrating to whack him when he just lies there so I whack at the birds but I keep missing so I whack his books and papers off the table and knock his chair down and scream extra long and he is sitting up and so I throw the stick at his head and I miss.

I scream a bit more and then another bit and then stop.

– Why didn't you tell me the cat would burn? I say.

He stares at me. He nods.

– My child, he says.

– I am not your child, I shout.

He nods again.

– Orla I told you the creatures must stay with me. The second life is with me or they must enter into the light of God.

– She didn't enter the light of God, I shout. – She burned on the grass.

Jesus nods again.

– She was taken into the light, he says.

I go out. Half the sky is pale and the sun is down. The midges are thick and birds are flitting from the barn. I head around the side and find the bones in the burnt grass and pick up two bird skulls and head back into the barn and hold them up at Jesus.

– What about these? I shout and throw them. – Were these taken into the light of God?

He starts to pull back his sleeve. I can see his arms are battered. I have opened some cuts.

– They have entered the light, he says. – But they may come back through the power of my blood.

And I see him reach for one of the skulls.

– No! I shout. – Don't do it! Don't do it!

He pauses.

– Don't.

He puts the skull down.

I sit across from him. It is getting darker really quickly.

I want him to speak but he just waits.

– There's no more phone, I say. – It is gone now. I won't be able to bring it again.

– Yes, he says.

My throat is dry and I just want to go home. But I can't bear the sight of Dad and definitely not Sue. And I don't want to cycle anymore. Or talk.

I don't know what to do.

There is nothing else to say.

His eyes are faint in the dark.

I scratch the earth.

After a bit I stand up.

I go out. Leave him and get my bike.

The night is moonless and the weir is dark and I think I might fall in if I try to take the bike across. Behind me there is a soft cooing from Daly's Barn and the air is midge thick and warm with the odd feather drifting past.

I am so tired.

I don't want it to just end like this.

I think I could fall asleep standing up.

The night air is cold through my shirt.

I could go.

But I can't.

I can't leave now.

I can hardly remember her face.

I walk back into the barn and push the bike into the wall. It falls with a bang and a cling.

Jesus is sat where I left him in the shadows.

– You owe me, I say.

He is silent.

– You ruined my escape and killed my cat. I am in worlds of trouble I wouldn't be in if it wasn't for you and it will be hard to get anywhere now and you owe me.

There is shuffling in the rafters above.

– What do you want Orla? he says.

I bite my lip.

– I want you to come with me to Ireland.

There is a long pause.

It is too long.

So I say it again.

– I want. I want you to come with me to Ireland. Come with me to Ireland and raise my mother back to life.

He pauses. Then he speaks.

– Ireland is very far away Orla.

– Yes. But there is a boat we can take. I have checked it out the price and everything. I will pay the ticket. I will pay it.

I wish I could see his face or even his shoulders. But he is not moving and his voice is quiet in the breezy silence without the light of the phone between us.

– You do not understand Orla. I have to bring the word of God to the world. Nothing is more important than this.

I can feel everything slipping away from me.

– No but you can start from Ireland that is where you should start. That is where they need God the most they are like really bad they are terrorists and paedophiles and you have to start there.

– Orla you don't understand. When I first came to Earth I came to Israel. Rome is the centre of the largest church. The greatest need is –

– No you have to come you have to come. You have to come. Come. You have to come. You owe me. You owe me.

He stands up and walks to the mouth of the barn and now he is kind of stiff and I have ruined everything.

I shouldn't have hit him.

I should have asked him earlier. Prepared him.

The sun has gone and he is a shadow on the sky and the way he stands is sore and I have fucking played this wrong.

– Wait, I shout and I run to the bushes and I nearly slip into the weir and I grab under the hedge where I stashed his clothes last night and I run back dropping socks and I throw the pile of T-shirts at him.

– You owe me. I gave you all these clothes from my father's house I washed them and cleaned them and brought them to you what are you going to do just walk to Roman Israel or wherever? Are you gonna go naked? They will arrest you for being naked that is stupid. Or in your blanket that is the same you will look like a moron they will not take you on a boat wearing a blanket! You need a boat! Have you thought of anything? Or are you gonna steal these clothes because that is what you will be doing. Trousers jeans T-shirts all stolen! From me! You said I should not steal but you are stealing if you take them and if you do not take them then you are just going to prison!

I am screaming at the end bending down picking up

T-shirts flinging them round him. Pants. Socks. The minging jeans. But Jesus does not move.

So I stop.

I stand looking at him.

Breath all mad.

– Please, I say. – Please.

He doesn't make a sound.

– It's my mother. Please.

I have a weird impression for a second I can feel the night growing behind me. The grass and trees. Canals. Nettles in the ditch. Clouds. Planets. The sky stretching upwards and outwards.

Until he speaks.

– Okay Orla. I will come with you.

The world snaps back into place.

– Right.

I look up. Look down.

– Okay. Okay. So. So you have to wait for me to come back.

He does not move.

– I might be a while. I'll be two days. I'll be two days and I'll leave my bike with you. You will be here in two days won't you?

I think he nods.

– Okay, I say.

He is coming to Ireland.

– You are coming to Ireland. Yes?

Pause.

His eyes twinkling. The smallest nod. In his throat a tiny grunt.

– Yes, I say. – You are coming. Yes.

If there is any chance of it working I need to leave my bike here. If I bring it back they will take it. So I leave it and look back once more at Jesus.

– Two days. I'll be two days.

I turn. Turn back. Turn again. Go.

I think he watches me go.

Tall shadow in the barn door.

Walking the path back is far slower than cycling but when I reach the dock no one is in the street and Dad's car is gone in the cul-de-sac. Sue is stood by the window and has the light on in the kitchen. I try to creep in but she is stood looking down the hallway at me with a fag in her mouth. Smoking inside our house. Phone in her hand.

– That's her now, she says into the phone.

I head upstairs. I want a drink but I am not walking past Sue so just suck it from the bathroom taps. I walk past Lily's room and there is a draft so I look in.

The blanket is off her. I check out her hands.

I can't see a mark.

I pull her blanket up over her and get into bed.

Five minutes later Sue opens my bedroom door. The light is on behind her but I keep my head down and pretend to be asleep. The whole house smells of cigarettes now.

Standing over me in the dark she says three things.

First, – He's out there looking for you now. Been out the whole bloody night. Called the cops and all.

I don't respond.

Next she says, –You know you have broken his heart. You have broken his heart and he does not deserve that.

I know I have. I don't care. My heart is broken too.

Last she says the obvious thing. The thing I knew was coming.

– Your mother would be so ashamed of you.

She waits. Trying to get a response. And normally I would give it to her hell for leather yes I would. Get up and slam things about and smash them and shout and wake Lily with the sound of breaking. Very good well played that wasn't very hard was it. But not tonight. Tonight I lie there and wait for Sue to leave without getting her thunder. Mum might be ashamed of the way I am going on but I am the only one doing anything and not pretending everything is going to be fine and she would know in her heart there is no way I can stop this now.

21

I wake up hungry. I don't have my phone but my Hello Kitty clock still works and says 7.50.

The house is breezy. There is clattering downstairs. I need a shower but I don't dare. I wash my pits and get my other uniform out of the press and double the deodorant.

Sue has all the windows open. She is bleaching the sponges and cloths and wringing them out on the draining board and does not turn as I come in. Lily is sat in her high-chair eating toast and Marmite cut into squares and a Tommee Tippee of orange juice.

– Orla! she says.

I get two Weetabix and put them down beside her and take her out of her chair to sit on my knee like a shield.

– Where you go last night Orla? she says.

– I had to go out for a walk Lily.

Lily nods. Sue grunts from the sink. I jig Lily on my knee and eat my Weetabix.

Sue turns to give me the stink eye. Sipping coffee with her rubber gloves still on.

– Your father came back at four, she says.

I sip some of Lily's orange juice.

– He'd got as far as Chorley. He's sleeping in now.

– Daddy still sleeping? says Lily.

Sue doesn't answer. I think about asking her where the boys are. Why not? Hey Sue why are you getting a divorce anyway? Like my dad much? Fancy moving in here saving his broken heart?

– Yes Daddy's still sleeping, I say.

– Poor Daddy all asleep, says Lily.

Sue whips off the gloves rolls them up and puts them on the windowsill. Pours the bleachy water from the basin down the sink. Turns round and glares while she opens a new pack of cigarettes. Pops one out and plays with it in her fingers.

– I am taking you to school. We leave in twenty minutes and I want you ready, she says.

Then she takes her cup and goes out the back door.

Lily rests her head against me and sucks on her toast as I finish my Weetabix. I get my bag ready brush my teeth and then sit in the living room and give Lily pigtails. Sue heads out at 8.25 and just sits in the car waiting for us. I want to ask if we are bringing Lily but then I just bring her. I can see Sue twitch as I unlatch Lily's car seat from our car and make a fuss over the seat belt and finally wrangle Lily in. I am glad that she twitches. I keep chatting to Lily all the way and I don't give Sue an edge to speak and we get to school right in the middle of the rush.

– Bye Orla, says Lily as I duck out into the crowd.

Form then Science. At Break I slide away from Zoe and head out to the back gate. I had a feeling and when I get there I see that I was right.

Sue's car is parked between the back gate and the front with a good view on both. Smoking a fag on her bonnet.

I think she nods at me.

She will be there at lunchtime too.

I could take somebody's coat. Zoe would give me her coat.

Sue might see me anyway.

I could go over the long drop.

Nobody goes over the long drop it is like death.

Bell goes and I head to English. Geography after. There has got to be some way out of this but I can't see it. Really I could go to sleep but my mind keeps ticking and my breath is edgy and I put my head back against the wall and pretend I am listening but this is mad.

I can't see what to do.

There was a time when I would have asked Jamie. Me and him were stone-cold killers. Mad dogs. Nothing would stop us.

I reckon he is my only shot.

Bell goes and I slip Zoe and head off down the pitches. Jamie is there. He gets free lunches but usually beeps his thumb for some other boy and they give him cash. Or he used to do that. Now he is sitting on his bag with a couple of boys from 9D watching Alfie B and a boy I don't know batter a ball about. I stand over up close and they go quiet. Jamie is eating a sausage roll out of a bag.

The others watch us.

– Jamie, I say.

He sniffs.

– Go away Orla.

– Jamie I need to talk to you.

He sniffs again.

The other boys start to grin and gurn. Alfie B stops kicking and the boy he is playing with shouts over, – Orla's got the horn, and the other boys burst out laughing. I feel my face going red and all down my chest and I want to die or run or smash him in the face. But all I can do is look at Jamie.

He has his mouth full.

But he shrugs and laughs.

– Look just go away, he says. – Just fuck off.

And that is that. Jamie is over.

And I will not cry in front of any of their stupid laughing faces and I turn and walk away and hear the hoots behind me and fuck the lot of them and then I see white.

It's a ball.

Someone has booted a ball into the back of my head.

For a second I can't see the tears are knocked out of me from pain but I am not sad all I feel is pure rage and if I had a gun I would go full massacre right now but I don't turn they will not see my face like this I just get up and walk past the fire escape and there is shouting behind me I don't care I just have to get around the corner and I do.

– Orla.

It is Jamie. He has run up breathless.

– Fuck off Jamie, I say.

We are behind the bins around the side but I will not let him see my face.

– It wasn't me Orla, he says. – That was Tommo he's a prick.

All I have is anger. I cannot even speak.

– I smacked him in the face. That was too much, he says.

I rub my temples. Get the tears off my face with the thumbs.

– But I told my ma I wouldn't talk to you, he says. – She says you burned me with the rap for Lemons's car. You hopped off scot-free and you will drag me down.

I nod.

He just stands there.

I glance out under my fringe.

– She's right, I say. – It shouldn't only have been you got done for the car. But I was away and that was that and there's nothing I can do about it. So just go.

He stares at me. Touches his thumb to his face.

– Stop looking at me and go!

I try to shout but my voice is all raspy.

– Go away Jamie, I say again.

I don't want him to go.

He stands there.

Starts to speak twice then he does.

– What did you want anyway? he says.

– My dad thinks I burned a cat, I say. – He thinks I burned a cat and he says he is going to get me help and he means get me taken away. The woman from the council is having the monthly meeting on Friday and Dad will tell them everything but last time they said he was under review and I think they will take me away.

He watches me.

Scratches his nose.

Jamie was in three different foster homes before his mum finally kicked his dad out for good. Two of them were proper bad.

He bites his lip and turns his back to the wall. Slides down it.

– Fuck.

He rubs his eyes.

Taps his head gently on the wall.

– What'll you do? he says.

– Just. Just. I don't know, I say.

He snorts.

– Still planning on going to Ireland? he says.

I nod.

– Just. I can't. He has Sue here. I can't do anything. They are watching everything.

He gets up and kicks the tarmac softly. Kicks the wall.

– What do you need? he says.

I shrug. – I don't know. I mean I do. But.

He grunts and nods.

– I need money. About one hundred quid. And a bike. A grown-up one gears and all. And food. For three days.

He bursts out laughing.

His face is hard again. He hoots and hops around but not like the old days when he was just being mad. It is like I just slapped him. He is saying I am crazy.

I watch him and feel my face twist again and look away.

– You are some kid Orla McDevitt. You are some kid.

– I need them.

He sways his head. Zip-zaps his arms so I am not sure he is going to dab or smack me in the mouth. Zips his hoody up and pulls down the toggles.

– You are some kid.

He walks away. Glances back. Walks away.

He will pull through for me. I am nearly sure of it.

22

Dad picks me up. He doesn't say anything just sits at the front of the queue. Daring me not to find him. I climb in the front and we drive home listening to his breathing.

Sue's car is still out front.

So when I get in I have worked out how to survive the evening. Rather than sit staring at each other I just play with Lily. We play Knock-the-Tower-Down and earn a, – Tidy up those bloody bricks once you've done, from Sue. We play Ninja-Who-Need-Not-See taking turns with the blindfold and rattling around the living room. Dad cooks oven pizzas while we play Hide-and-Seek and Sue phones her boys in the hallway keeping an eye on the front door as we charge up and down the stairs.

She needn't have bothered though. Not tonight.

After pizza I announce I need a bath and Lily says she wants to come in with me which we haven't done for like a year. I am a bit freaked out but it is better than Sue coming in for a woman-to-woman so I meet Dad's eyes and he nods.

It is lovely having the bath with Lily.

At first I just want to scrub my body and sit but Lily has to sit on my knees because it is too hot and she goes through all the names of the kids at her table in playgroup but making up stupid names like Mr Bee and Mr Breakfast then doing her funny joke laugh. Then I do her hair with no shampoo in her eyes for the second time. Then we just sit covering our hands with shampoo and trying to blow bubbles with our fingers.

– Now I am going to dry my hair, she announces.

And she climbs out the side of the bath and I dry her with a beach towel but she wants one around her hair like Mum used to do for me and I climb dripping out of the bath and do it with a hand towel and hold her up to the mirror and she nods.

– That's right, she says.

Then she goes downstairs to get Dad to dry her hair and I nearly follow her but I don't want the hassle. So I get back in but the water is cold now and soon enough Sue opens the door and I cover my boobs because we never got a lock on this room as we have always been a house that knocks. And Sue says, – Wipe that floor before you come down and don't leave it for anyone else.

I don't curse at her.

I get up after a few minutes wipe the floor and go in and put on my jim-jams. I get my gym bag and put in two pairs of fresh leggings and two pairs of knickers and two bras and an extra vest and two tops and some tampons and a hairbrush and my inhaler just in case and get my toothbrush and put that in too.

Everything doubled. One for the journey one for the ferry.

If Jamie pulls through for me.

Then I zip up my bag and leave it by the bedroom door and head down.

Lily is still putting on her tears as Dad brushes the knots out of her hair but she has her juice and *Blue Planet* is on the telly and then we watch the fish against the sound of the hairdryer. Soon it is time for Lily's bed and she comes and gives us all a hug. Dad and Sue and me. And I wish Sue would go out for a fag while we hug as it is a family moment.

– Na-night Orla.

– Na-night Lily.

As Dad takes her up I stick on the hairdryer full volume. Sue tries to talk to me twice but I pretend not to hear. I dry and dry it until my scalp is sore and then Sue heads upstairs and I turn it off and keep watching the fish.

Stripy fish.

A multicoloured squid.

I think of Jesus swimming past basking sharks whose mouths look like ribcages.

Dead bodies in a box under the sea.

I can't stay long or they will corner me in front of the telly.

So I head to my room and Sue is going through my gym bag.

– Why do you need two pairs of everything? she says.

I don't speak. Just reach in lift the tampons and jiggle them about and drop them in.

Sue rolls her eyes and throws in the two bras. And I walk past her and get the play we are reading in English and pretend to read it.

When she leaves I close the door after her. I go straight to the lower bookshelf with the Roald Dahls and Artemis Fowls and pull out *Traffic-Free Cycle Paths in the Northwest*.

I practically know it by heart. I have thumbed it so many times and jotted notes on the edges that if anyone found it the whole game would be up. But nobody ever picks it up or even sees it. Mum bought it for Dad's birthday back in 2012.

Still got her handwriting on the first page.

Happy Birthday Tubby – On your bike!

Getting to Preston should be fine but it might be tricky finding the Ribble Link. But if I can get on the Ribble Link it should be plain sailing to Liverpool. It was always going to be hard with no phone but with Jesus we will have to go at night. If my maths is right it is 65.2 miles which could take three nights if we are doing it all in the dark.

If we get a bike.

If we can't get a bike it could take us a week of walking.

With no food and no cash.

So much depends on Jamie.

Sue goes out that night for a smoke at 10 and at 11.15 and at 12.30. Each time she heads out Dad knocks on my door. The third time he comes in I have the light off and I lie there pretending to sleep as he says my name with his hand hovering over my shoulder.

23

The money turns out to be the easiest.

In the morning eating breakfast Lily gets it into her head she wants to come into school with me again. Dad is sleeping in and Sue says no but Lily starts crying until Sue gives in. Unhappily. Good girl Lily. Her car seat is back in Dad's car so Sue has to wrestle it out but does not have the knack of it. I literally offer to help but she growls at me, – I can do it, and marches me by the arm to the front seat of her car and throws her handbag in my lap. Then goes over to Lily's car seat humphing and grunting.

Dad has far more sense than to leave money around me but honestly I am sitting there staring at her purse on top of her cigarettes. I almost feel bad taking it but she doesn't even look as I slip a handful of notes – not all of them I am not stupid – into my pocket while she makes a mess of putting Lily's belt on.

– You could have bloody helped, says Sue when she gets in and whips the bag off me for keys.

– Sorry, I say.

When we stop I lean back and give Lily an awkward hug.

– Bye Orla.

– Bye Lily.

She is still sucking a corner of toast. I squeeze her and then head into school. And straight in to the toilets to check my pocket.

Two twenties and a tenner.

It's better than nothing.

Won't get me two on the ferry though.

I put it in my bumbag under my shirt.

Form then RE. Dawkins keeps smiling at me. I am clicking a pen in my hand the whole time. Zoe shows me her new trainers. Then it is break and I am in the yard walking around trying to find Jamie. He is not in the pitch and he is not by the bins. But I see him near reception just after the bell goes and shuffle up to him.

He shakes his head.

My heart pops.

– Jamie, I say.

But there is a light in his eye.

It is the look he had before we shot up Lemons's car.

And he grins and leans in and whispers, – Find me at lunch.

Double science. We are cutting flowers looking for plant parts. I pretend to take notes by writing *xylem* and *phloem* at the top of the page and underlining them again and again. Hanniway sees but says nothing.

I can't settle.

Jamie must have got something.

When the bell goes he is outside the class. He nods and tilts his head and I follow him past Food Science through a babbling crowd of year sevens. We get to the disabled toilet and wait for a year twelve to pass and check the corridor and when no one is looking we head in.

– Jamie I. I just wanted. Listen.

He squints at me.

– Listen. I mean your mum. She's. I know. I know she's right. I should have got half the rap.

He blinks and sniffs at me.

– I couldn't get much money, he says.

He holds out a hand.

Two fivers. Crumpled.

– That's all she had in her purse.

I can't.

She will kill him.

He jerks his hand.

– Go on.

– Jamie. I can't.

– Go on, he says. – They didn't do me for the car anyway. They did me for the phones.

He is going to get it for this. I know it.

But I need it. That will be sixty quid. Enough for two singles on the ferry and two quid left over.

I take it and slip it in my bumbag.

Then he puts his bag on the toilet and opens it.

– You like the chicken wraps isn't it, he says.

And he takes out four Boots chicken wraps and two club sandwiches and puts them on the cistern. Then he puts a large bottle of Dr Pepper and a stack of Refresher bars in the sink.

– They only had four wraps so I got you something else big, he says. – The drink and the bars are just from the house.

I look at all the food and I feel like crying. And I want to reach out and touch him but that would be weird so I look away.

– Thanks, I say.

He nods at me.

So I pack it in my schoolbag. The Dr Pepper only fits in my gym bag. Then he says, – Come on let's get the bike.

– You got a bike? I say.

– Yeah I got a bike.

– How?

He closes his eyes and goes full Pikachu grin.

– Come on I'll show you.

So he leads me downstairs to the ground floor labs and we pass a few stragglers heading to the canteen. He nods at me to wait and then saunters past the lab techs' door and turns and tries the handle and gives me the nod.

We go through the lab techs' room and it is empty and that opens on to Chemistry which is Lemons's lab and then down the back of that into the storage room. In the storage room there is a fire escape and a computer and a bike.

It is blue with TREK written on the side. There is quite a bit of mud up it but twenty-seven gears and a bell and a light.

It is not chained to anything.

I am wide eyed. I turn to Jamie. He is grinning madly.

– Saw it the other day.

He starts laughing.

– He must have got it after we shot his car up. The prick.

I am laughing too.

– But – why has he not got it chained?

Jamie shrugs.

I mean nobody can get in here without passing Lemons or a room of lab techs.

Unless they have all gone to lunch.

Jamie tests the fire escape with his shoulder and it is not hooked up to the alarm and it opens. There are loads of fag butts here and it smells of fags. Jamie kicks at the butts.

– Lemons smokes I reckon, he says.

I wheel the bike backwards past the computer chair and through the door passing close to Jamie as he holds it open. Out beside a big blue bin in a nook off the staff car park.

– You just need to head out the main drive as the back gate will be manned, he says. – If you are quick they will be at lunch.

That's not true. Sue could be out the front.

Or my dad.

But if I wait the techs will definitely come back.

I will not get this chance again.

I turn to Jamie and I think I am about to kiss him. It is not right that I got away with the car I got a gold pass with my mum just dead. But Jamie helped me and he has always been my best friend and he is smaller than me by just a bit but his skin isn't even bad now and he is looking at me and he is going to get it for this and I don't know where to put my hands so I tug at the straps of my bag and tighten my gym bag at my waist.

– I better go now, he says, – before the techs get back.

And he kind of slouches and moves his foot and before I can say anything the door is closing. I call after. I say, – Jamie, and he turns and grins and leans up against the glass.

– Mothafucka, he says. – Mothafucka.

I laugh.

– Mothafucka, I say.

He nods. Grins wide. Blinks.

Then he turns and heads back through the lab.

Jamie is gone.

Jamie the mad dog.

I wish I had kissed him.

But I didn't.

I guess I better go too.

Bumbag.

Sixty quid.

Wraps.

Dr Pepper.

No knife.

No phone.

Two bags.

I get on the bike. The handles feel new. It is bigger than mine the seat a touch too high but I manage the second time. I wheel it slowly to the edge of the nook.

Dawkins is at the far side of the drive. I guess it is him on duty but he is chatting to Dolores at Reception not looking my way so I just go for it. I pedal slow all cool cool not doing anything wrong and get off at the barrier and don't look back just wheel it around cool cool and no one calls out. At the front gate I look left and there is Sue's car down a bit but I can't see her so I don't wait I just pedal into town and I don't hear anything behind me and I am at the roundabout and now wheeling down towards Tesco's and here is the towpath and now I am free.

24

It is a sunny day. There are a couple of dog walkers on the canal path and I reckon my shirt and tie are a dead giveaway. I can't dump my uniform here in case they find it and work out I am on the towpaths. Or think I am drowned in the canal which is a laugh because I could stand up in it.

But I don't want them thinking I am dead.

So I stop and take off the tie and ruffle the shirt so it looks like a top and put the hoodie in the gym bag and hang the bag off the handlebars so I am not all cluttered and hot. Anybody could see the skirt is a school skirt but not which school.

The sun is warm on my face and forearms. It is sweaty work and under the rucksack my back is soaking. But there is no one around as I go under the third bridge and the sunlight reflects all shimmery onto the underside of the bridge and the breeze is lovely through the gaps in my shirt.

I hoot a little.

Just a little. When there is no one near.

I don't dare use the roads now as this is the last minute when they are most likely to get me. When I get to Daly's Barn I cross the weir and go in quietly.

There are birds in the rafters. Small green shoots push out of the stone in the shadows. Ducks and crows sit on the crumpled body of Jesus in a far corner from the daylight at the door. The birds rustle as I come near. He has an arm over his face like he is dabbing.

I can see the marks on his arm where I battered him.

I shudder but I shake it off.

His beard has grass in it and his clothes are filthy with grass stains and birdshit. I go to the pile of clothes on the table and sniff a T-shirt.

It's bad.

We will need to wash them before the ferry and I think about taking them to the canal and having a go now but anyone could be walking a dog on a day like this. We can wash them near Liverpool where no one knows me.

There are still some things to do though. I check Jesus is asleep then get changed in the shadows. Leggings and a T-shirt from my gym bag and then I empty a plastic bag of books and put my uniform in it. I spend a few minutes trying to chuck the bag onto the rafters and the pigeons are not happy then I hit one knocking it off its place and it flies for the door.

The second it hits the beam of sunlight it flashes into fire.

Feathers alight. An odd squeal in its throat. Falling ablaze in a short arc to the ground.

I duck low and grunt.

There is a pigeon burning in the barn doorway.

No noise no scream anymore just the quiet crackle of flame.

I rush to see if anyone is on the path.

There's nobody there.

So I get the stick I used to batter Jesus and poke the pigeon back into the barn and the flames die after I whack it for a bit. But it smells rank. The barn fills with meaty smoke and I keep gagging. The birds in the rafters grumble but don't fly near the door and I don't blame them. I roll a boulder over on to the burning pigeon and think of Sneaky and hope nobody sees smoke from the path.

Fuck.

But there is no one walking the path.

And the smoke dies down.

Stinks. But dies down.

Poor poor Sneaky. Her last moments.

Burning in the light.

They will think I am mad if they find another burned animal.

After a while I climb on Jesus's table and slot my uniform up onto a high ledge and that will have to do because I can't do any better. Then I take out Jamie's food and lay it on Jesus's books. I try one of the club sandwiches and it is rank just a dry triple-decker sandwich but at least it is big and then I have one Refresher bar and two small sips of Dr Pepper.

I have to make it all last.

Then I split the food and clothes into two piles. My schoolbag is bigger than my gym bag and if we take half the sandwiches each he can take the Dr Pepper and we can each take our own clothes. I leave the schoolbooks and other crap of course except *Traffic-Free Cycle Paths in the Northwest* and we will have to leave Jesus's extra jumper but I stand on the desk and slot what we don't need up next to my uniform.

The rest fits in the two bags.

– Jesus, I say. – Are you asleep?

No movement.

If I drag him into the light will he burn too?

He doesn't snore.

I can hardly hear him breathe.

But I think we are ready to go. I sit with my back to the warm stone doorway reading *Traffic-Free Cycle Paths* again and the day is so warm that at some point I must have fallen asleep. Because when I wake the air is half-blue and midgey and Jesus is stood looking out into the early night.

Tall and skinny and quiet.

– That's your bike, I say.

He turns.

I wave at Lemons's bike on the wall.

– Did you steal it? he says.

I nod but he isn't looking at me.

– Did you steal it?

– Yes I did.

He goes to it. Touches it. Rings the bell once.

– You should not steal Orla.

I stretch and stand feeling the marks of the stone on my back.

– I have told you this before.

– Yes but we need a way to get to Liverpool don't we?

His back is to me.

– Liverpool, he says. – You know how to get there?

– Yes. I have a book.

He sighs.

– You want to see it? All the way to Liverpool. Avoiding the roads. Out of sight. Until we get to the ferry.

I reckon we could have another argument now so I pick *Traffic-Free Cycle Paths* up off the ground and open it to the map and pass it over but Jesus only shakes his head. So I stuff the book in my bag while he stares at the sky or God-knows-what and I pick up his bag and wave it at him until he takes it. Then I take my bike by the handlebars and wheel it out of the barn.

The stars are coming out.

Jesus follows me slowly.

Watching me as I move.

– We have to go, I say. – Soon. I mean. Now. Get on your bike.

He doesn't get on.

– Show me once more how it is done, he says.

Of course.

Maybe he has never ridden a bike.

25

So I show him.

I take the bag off him and put it down with mine in the barn. Then I lead him to the middle of the field and I get up on my bike and show him how to work the brakes. Turn on his light for him. A crescent moon is rising low and bright and he watches me wheeling through the grass the long stems whipping my spokes. Grass is harder to ride on than road it pushes back and you can't see the dips and it is just more work to pedal through. But I remember from being a kid it makes you less afraid of falling and anyway we can't practice on the road so here it is.

I brake and turn to watch him try.

– Your go, I say. – Just do that.

He sits up straight on the bike and lifts both his legs and topples over to one side.

I burst out laughing.

He is so long and gangly even on the big bike. I come off mine and stand behind him. He is massively tall up close and smells like soil and sweat. But I tell him again how to sit and not to look down. I try to remember the things Mum told me when I was learning. How she held the back of the seat and ran with me and pushed.

– Don't be afraid of falling, I say. – The grass is soft.

– I am not afraid, he says.

And he does fall. Twice more into the dirt he loses balance and collapses half-catching himself with his leg before toppling like a slow tree. Then he pulls the brakes too fast and flips over the handlebars into the grass with the bike rolling on top of him. Each time he falls I laugh so much I pee myself a little. I know he is impatient to get going and I think the second time he fell he got badly hurt as he limped when he got up but he does not get annoyed at my laughing and just smiles.

But I mean it is pretty funny.

So we try again. I grab the back of his seat and push. He brakes. And we try again and again.

I cannot support his weight as I run alongside him because he is a grown man and so if he wobbles I have to let go. And I cannot hold his back like a parent because I don't want him leaning on me. But I can hold the back of his seat and tell him to kick off the ground with the back foot and press on the pedal with the front and to keep the front foot higher as he launches. And literally it is only about the ninth time he manages to do it. I let him go and he goes sailing over the grass. Whipping his own path through the long stems. I hoot slightly as he wobbles but straightens the wheel and loops and cycles around me. He goes faster and faster and then slows a bit too close to me and then stops.

But he stops right.

I mean he wobbled a bit but just a bit.

From how bad he started it is amazing.

– You really are the Son of God, I say laughing.

He laughs too.

For a second it seems we could just hang out here.

But no we have to go so I straighten up.

– Look, I say. – Do you think you can manage it along the cycle path? I mean we can take it slowly. It will be narrow and you will have to balance and if you don't you will fall in the water.

Jesus looks down at the handlebars and wobbles them and pulls the brakes.

– Are you going first? he says.

– I can go first, I say. – We just need to keep the lights on.

He swings his leg off the bike. Swings it back on.

Pulls on the brakes again.

– Yes I think I can do that.

So I head into the barn the last time and get the bags and pass him his. Tell him how to hang the gym bag on his shoulder so it doesn't bang into his knees when he pedals but he works it out straight away. Then I strap my own bag on and pull it tight and I tell him to follow me and we walk the bikes across the weir until we are on the side of Cooper's Ridge with Glasson Dock's lights on the horizon.

Jesus comes close after me. His old ratty blanket around his shoulders like a cape.

– Are you ready? I say.

Jesus nods.

– Are you really wearing that?

– Yes, he says.

I shrug.

So we head off up towards Galgate in the fairly bright light of the crescent moon. I check behind to see he is still there but he keeps coming not wobbling too badly and so I face forward and push on.

26

I reckon it takes like an hour to the main Lancaster Canal. It is dark and the mud so bumpy and cracked from the dry dry week I have to stop to push the bike up the steep weirs. But the air is warm and the countryside smells of dung and flies.

But when we hit the main canal the path widens and the climb is easier. We pass Potter's Brook and leave the A6 behind and then it feels like we could be anywhere at all. There is a panicky moment when I scare a heron out of the bushes and she lifts up past me and another one lifts up a moment after right through the light of my bike light.

I stop a second to catch my breath.

I have never gotten this far south before. Not on my own.

Jesus catches up. He looks as the herons settle across the canal. I hold up a hand against the glow of his bike light.

– How's the bike? I say.

– It's fast, he says. – Much faster than walking.

– We just keep on this path, I say. – Follow it through a bunch of villages until we get to Preston then we split to the Savick Brook.

– It says that in the book? he says.

I grunt.

– Can I go first? he says.

I grunt again. And he fixes the gym bag and carefully adjusts his footing on the pedals and then heads off in front of me.

This way lets us bypass the roads. The book says it is scenic and peaceful. I guess in the day you could see sheep and hills. Most of what I see is shades of black against the lighter black of the sky. Sometimes there are fields on one side and sometimes trees on both sides and in front a cone of light the moths tap in and out of. There are tree roots on the track. Fallen branches I don't want caught in my spokes. We pass a caravan park. A bunch of boats. Then nothing but trees and shades of black again.

Stars reflect on the water. Part of me thinks we could be going in the wrong direction. But eventually we come to what I reckon must be the Garstang Marina.

There are loads of boats with people chatting on them and streetlights and the sky opens up. I know there is supposed to be a pub and I see the sign The Ow'd Tithe Barn and I know I came the right way and I am happy. Across the water there's a beer garden with a few tables full of drinking men. I slow down behind a tree.

– Jesus, I whisper.

He mustn't hear me and just keeps going.

– Jesus, I hiss louder.

If anything I reckon he pedals faster.

So I hop on the bike and leg it after him. And it is the length of Garstang before I catch up breathlessly whipping past nettles and in and out of the orange streetlights.

I cannot believe he is so fast. For a second my stomach goes watery and I think he is running away but finally when the last light of the village is behind I see his dark lanky shape up ahead at a crook in the water.

– What was, I say. – What was that for?

He waits for me to catch my breath.

– You said we would stay out of sight, he says.

– I did but.

I spit in the water. Hold my knees.

– I did but we will lose each other if you pile on like that.

We stand watching the moon as my breath grows quieter.

– You said it is just one path. So we cannot lose one another unless one of us turns off.

– Yes but.

– But what?

I don't know but what.

– Do not worry Orla, he says. – I have walked these lanes a long time now. I will not leave you behind.

He is right of course. I know he is. But we are miles and miles from Preston and I am already hungry. He gets out the Dr Pepper and we both have a drink. I offer him a Refresher bar and he says no so I fold it up on itself twice put the whole thing in my mouth and we cycle on as I suck in the sugary juice.

I am a bit pissed off. With him I mean. He keeps cycling ahead and now he is waiting for me at every bridge. I am supposed to be faster cycling is my thing. But he has those big gangly legs and his breathing comes easy.

But I need him now.

To raise Mum.

It is hard to stop thinking about her.

Usually I just stop thoughts of her. It's like shut up just shut up plan the trip make a list google train times whatever. But now we are on the actual trip it is harder to shut her out of my mind.

So I try to think about Dad looking for me. Wondering how far he'll get. If the cops are looking for me yet. If Sue is staying over on the sofa. Or my room? His room? Hey Sue why are you getting divorced anyway? I get too angry thinking about that but then I go back to thinking about Mum and that's no better so I try to think about the path the stones the roots the moths but that works for like two minutes so then I think about being hungry instead.

That works pretty well as I am really really hungry.

We pass through Bilsborrow and it is like Garstang. Streetlights and boats and a pub. The pub is empty now though. Still Jesus pegs it away from the lights and I lose sight of him until the far side of the village where he is stood holding out the Dr Pepper.

– You really don't, I say. – You really don't like pubs do you?

I think he nods.

– That place, I say. – It was. It was empty.

Nothing.

– Did you not see. The car park?

– Pubs are dangerous, he says. – They can be violent places.

I sip the Dr Pepper. But as I drink I start to chuckle and get it up my nose and spit it out in a spluttery laugh.

– How, I say when I can breathe, – how can you be the Son of God when you can't even talk to people in a pub?

He doesn't respond. Just closes the Dr Pepper and puts it in his bag and cycles off.

And I know I was nasty but I am starving and tired.

The book says it should be eight hours from Galgate to the Ribble Link and back. So obviously one way it should only take three and a half maybe four. Half of fifty-seven miles is twenty-eight and a half so seven miles an hour. I am often faster than that around Glasson. But this feels a lot longer. Like more than three hours now and we are not at Preston yet.

The hunger is really annoying.

My bum is sore and so are my thighs.

Eventually I catch up with Jesus on the far side of a bridge and call out to him to stop. He pedals back to me. I get off the bike and sit down on the wet grass.

– I need to eat.

He looks back then leans his bike against the side of the bridge and turns off his light.

– No leave the light on, I say.

– They will see us from the road, he says.

– Not at this time of the night.

He pauses a second then turns it on pointed right down to make a pool of light on his front wheel. Then he sits beside me tucking his blanket under his butt. By my reckoning we are just down from The Hand and Dagger – but Jesus can't see it from here so won't kick up a fuss. Anyway it will definitely be empty now.

If I am right we are not far from Preston.

The grass is soaking into my butt but at least I have my hoodie.

I take a chicken wrap out.

– You hungry?

Jesus nods and I hand him the second club sandwich.

– Try this, I say. – I have had one of these already.

His hands stay in his lap.

– Will you have enough food for the whole trip? he says.

There are three wraps left.

I nod.

He takes his sandwich. Unwraps it carefully like he was undoing a nappy. I watch him pick out a piece of egg and smell it. Test it out on the tip of his tongue.

I laugh.

– Would you really rather eat some bloody uncooked duck?

He chews the sandwich considering it and then shakes his head.

– No, he says. – This is good too.

I laugh again. Then I chew for a bit. Thinking.

– How can you. I mean. How do you eat them? Do you cook the birds after you kill them?

Jesus shrugs in the darkness tearing off fragments of bread and popping them in his mouth.

– I have. When I can hide the fire. But even raw the meat or the blood can keep me going for days.

For a second I think I am about to throw up. Thinking of the skin on a bird's neck. I put the food down in my lap. But I am starving and this will pass.

– Last year before winter I ate berries too, he says. – And in spring there are eggs in the nests.

I think of the texture of uncooked egg. The crunch of egg-shell between my teeth.

I am a minute looking at the water until I can eat.

With no phone between us the silence feels weird.

– So why are you hiding anyway? I say.

Jesus coughs.

– Like shouldn't you be like praying and telling people what to do instead of hiding from people?

It takes him a moment to swallow.

– There will be time for that Orla. But I might well ask you the same question. Why are you hiding?

I blink and take a bite as my stomach settles.

– I stole a bike. And my dad might get me.

– You should not steal Orla. I have told you this before. And you should honour your father and mother.

– What about you, I say. – If your dad wants to take you into the light shouldn't you like just let yourself burn up in the sun?

He stops eating.

I think I hear him growl softly.

– But I am trying to honour my mother, I say. – I am trying to get her back to life and that is the greatest honour there is isn't it?

I can hear his breathing.

– I mean how long have you been wandering around here?

There is a long pause. But his breath softens and he takes a bite.

– Less than one year, he says after he swallows.

– And you weren't just battered in one pub were you?

In the half-light I cannot see his eyes.

– Battered means beaten up, I say.

– I know what battered means. But how did you know I was attacked more than once?

I shrug.

– I can see it in the way you act.

He nods. Chews and swallows.

– Three times. Three times I have tried to approach mankind. The first I told you about. The second time a man hit me with his head before I reached the pub door. And the third time I did get in. I talked to some people. But they laughed at me and told me I knew nothing.

I snort.

– I mean the blanket isn't normal. If you are going to talk to people you need to dress like them. Not some kind of hobo.

And maybe it is good without the phone. Because as we sit there he tells me more about his life. Hiding from late-night taxis. How he used to hunker down in the roadside bushes all night for enough light to read. How everything changed when he found his crappy garden light in a skip.

It all sounds pretty cold and lonely.

I kind of feel sorry for him.

Only kind of though.

But kind of.

I mean if he really is Jesus that means he cannot die.

Not really. Not like we die.

He knows he will rise again. Like for sure.

Not like Mum. Just waiting for the end.

But I don't say this.

Instead I say, – No but listen. It will be better next time. You just need to copy people. Dress like them. The blanket is the problem.

– I need the blanket, says Jesus. – For the mornings.

– Okay so just leave the blanket behind when you talk to people. Hide it like up a tree. My dad's jeans and T-shirts are a million miles better even covered with bird crap. At least you won't get chucked out before you get in.

He is quiet after we eat.

Maybe he is tired. I am. My butt is cold from the ground and my eyes feel gritty. But there is no time to rest.

No we are finished eating and I say it is time to go.

27

I think we must nearly be at Preston. It would be good to at least get to the Ribble before sunrise. So we pack up the food and drink and although I could just fall asleep on the wet grass we get the bikes upright and head off.

The sky looks to be brightening and soon to our right there is a train and I think we must be on the right path. There is mist low over the water. The first birds start. But eventually also to the right I see a huge athletics pitch which must be the university which means we have not missed a step.

I could nearly hoot but I am too tired.

The air is really cold now. I can see my breath. We have to leave the canal and cross an actual road called Tom Benson Way. I thought we would mess this bit up but we don't. There are still no cars about. Then we head under a bridge leaving the Lancaster Canal for the Savick Brook and the first weir goes down which means we are heading to the sea.

It is light enough to see statues along the way and we are picking up speed and I feel awake again. We leave the brook and pass a church and I laugh because Jesus is behind me on a bike not on a cross in the church and we pass another weir and then a field then another weir. We are leaving the air of Preston behind and I give a small howl as the day brightens grey around us.

– Orla.

He is calling but it would be a pity to stop before the we reach the Ribble. And his long legs can keep up with mine. But the path goes narrower and narrower which is weird and then he calls again.

– Orla.

I am not sure this is right anymore. So I turn and Jesus is pedalling after me with the blanket flowing behind him but something is wrong. He is finding it hard which is weird because he kept up all night and was faster than me for most of it. But as he pulls beside me I see his face.

His eyes are all shrivelled.

The grey sky of dawn is getting brighter.

It nearly looks like the light is inside him. Like a torch in a fist.

– I have to get out of the sun, he says.

And then he pedals off where the path is no more than a dent in the grass. And the birds are mad noisy and there is a forest before us. The ground is uneven and then we have to chuck the bikes over a fence.

– Jesus, I say.

He doesn't turn but I see half his face from behind.

His face is bad.

Skullface.

There is another fence and then we are in the forest. And I hurt my arm coming over the fence and now my second wind is gone and I just want to catch my breath. But Jesus is not even riding the bike anymore just pushing it through sticky thistles and ferns and I struggle to keep up.

Then he flings the bike down like an eight-year-old and dives onto the ground.

When I catch up he is a wreck. He is lying in a ditch pulling the blanket around his neck. The gym bag chucked beside him. His face is a scabby mess.

– Jesus?

He tugs the blanket over his head and is silent.

I kneel down. He is in a muddy dip below a bush. You might not see him from a distance.

I look around.

I guess not many people come this way. There is no path.

– Jesus?

I feel sick now. In my gut.

He doesn't answer. I peek under the blanket.

All scabs and his eyes are wet and sore.

It looks like there is steam coming off him.

It must be a trick of the light.

I tuck the blanket back and right his bike against a tree.

Then I stand for a minute and put my bike beside his.

There's nobody around.

I bend over. For a second I think I am about to throw up.

But nothing comes.

The birds are not as loud here and the plants are thick. My leggings keep snagging in sticky thistles. But I wander up and down to find the Savick Brook.

My head is really sore.

The forest is wrong. It makes no sense. There should be

a path by the water. There has to be. But when I get to the brook the bank is nothing but ferns and brambles.

I can see the sunlight start to glitter on the leaves.

I feel awful.

Headache headache headache.

I find a rowboat on the bank. There are two life jackets in it and a cushion at the back and the bottom is dry. I get in and lie down and then I am asleep.

28

I wake up and I know something is wrong.

It is horribly hot. I push the cushion around the floor of the boat and wrap my legs around a life jacket. But I can't settle. My thighs are sore from the bike and the boat is too hard but worse than that is the heat. Even under the leaves I am sweating and I can see daylight glowing pink through my eyelids.

I have no way of knowing the time.

Headache headache headache.

I am so thirsty.

I know I need sleep but the thirst gets me up stumbling through the trees. At first I have no idea of how the world fits together but then I see the colours of the gym bag and there's our bikes and there's Jesus. I have a brief crazy notion of tugging the blanket off him.

Of course I don't actually do it.

Instead I get the Dr Pepper. We only have half a bottle left. My throat is so dry I could down it all but I only take a quarter of what's left.

I spend ages just staring at things. There is mud up my leggings. My pits stink like old gym clothes. I have a long bloody scratch the entire length of my forearm and no idea where it came from. But it takes me a while on the dry leaves until I work out what is wrong.

Where is the path?

We are supposed to be following the canal path. *Traffic-Free Cycle Paths* shows them all the way down to Liverpool.

But there is no path here.

I head to the boat. The path must be on the other side of the canal. But I see nothing across from me but mudbanks and further up bushes.

Downstream just trees.

My side is all reeds.

I must be wrong so I get the book out. But it is clear as day. Route 18 is Galgate to the Ribble Link all the way up to Savick Brook. Then route 19 is The Ribble to Liverpool and starts on the other side. The two paths touch each other on the main map a dotted green line for 18 a continuous yellow line for 19. They must join up.

Unless they do not join up.

Why would they touch on the map if they do not join up?

But why are they different colours?

Why would the stupid author of a stupid cycle book show you two paths touching if the cycle paths don't fucking join up?

My belly goes watery.

I lie down in the boat.

Part of me wants to cry.

But it can't be true. I don't believe it. I have to see it so I walk off along the bank through the ferns with the book.

The forest does not last long. Maybe ten minutes through it I come to a small path and a restaurant with a playground.

The Lea Gate on my map. Five cars in the car park then a road with a bridge over the canal. I want to go in and buy a drink but they'll see my face so I just dash the road and climb the fence and I'm on the other side.

It is so hot I can nearly hear the sun buzzing. When I was a kid on a walk and I got tired Mum would take my hand and sing *Row Row Row the Boat*. If that didn't work she would show me bugs under a log. She told me once that dragonflies can't walk and their legs are just for landing.

She knew loads about insects.

I guess now the insects have eaten her.

We will have to dig her up.

Like Sneaky. All leathery gunk and bones.

No. Just two months in the ground now. Two and a bit. Not like Sneaky.

Not yet.

But there will be bugs.

Living hungry bugs.

In her eyes.

Crap like this keeps happening. Thoughts of Mum. Horrible thoughts. But the day is so hot I try to just focus on sheltering my head with the book. At least it has some fucking use. But eventually the muddy path flattens and the brook joins the River Ribble stretching brown and green before me.

There is very obviously no way across the river because it is a fucking river and you need a bridge to cross a river and the only bridges near here are back up in Preston.

I am so fucking stupid.

A small motor boat with three Union Jacks goes past me

towards Preston. An old woman is driving it with a small dog and she waves as they pass.

The dry muddy bank could be the surface of a brown moon.

I step into the mud. Nearer the water it cracks underfoot to a thick greeny brown. Like in Morecambe. The quicksand. Where the sand turns to mud and you could get sucked in and drown and they would have to dig you up.

We will have to dig up Mum.

Bugs in her eyes.

I head up back to the forest. Cover my head and shut out my thoughts and work through to the boat.

I mean it is obvious what we have to do. We have to go into Preston to cross the river. Which means working out how to get through the city and join the cycle path on the other side. But we will stick out like sore thumbs. I will need to use my clean ferry clothes just to not look like a zombie and there is a chance Dad could find us if he is in Preston.

My head aches. Aches.

I try screaming in the forest.

It does nothing.

I throw the book into a tree.

It just falls on the leaves.

I'll need the maps. I pick it up again.

I wish my head wasn't this sore.

Sip Dr Pepper.

The boredom is nearly as bad as the thirst.

I have not spent so long without a phone since I was a kid. It is really hard to keep your thoughts under control without it. No telly nothing to shut out my own mind. The book is no good because I know it and anyway it lied to me. So whatever way I turn there is nothing to stop me thinking about Mum.

Woodlice.

Leathery gunk.

Two months is not the same as two years. Two months is short.

I try to plan more.

How will we get from the ferry to Drumahoe? Will Sinead pick us up if I call her from Belfast? There is no way she can say no but what if she does?

But whatever I try it keeps coming back to Mum.

What will I say when Jesus lifts her?

Woodlice.

Eyeholes.

She will be so angry at me.

Roaring.

Insects in her mouth.

I will have to dig her out of the earth.

Like Sneaky wet bones and leather and gunk.

I don't lose control of my breath.

But I get really tired trying to close my thoughts.

Eventually I try a chicken wrap. It is warm and squished and I am so so hungry but I can barely touch the slime of it.

At some point I fall asleep on my gym bag.

29

When I wake Jesus is waving the bottle at me. For a second I don't know who he is but then I smell the meaty dust of his blanket.

I take just a tiny sip.

It is still twilight. Not fully dark. I sit upright and I am dreading saying it but it can't wait. So in a crotchety voice I say, – I got the path wrong.

I tell him the book lied and Ribble Link is a link for boats not bikes even though it's in a book for bikes. Tell him that we have to go into Preston to cross the river and I have no idea where because Preston is like a massive city and cities are not in *Traffic-Free Cycle Paths* because obviously there is traffic in a city.

But we have to.

And I am frightened he is going to get mad. But instead he gets up and fixes his blanket around him with the gym bag and stands beside his bike. He has my bike leant against the tree.

– Let's check the river, he says. – There must be a way across.

I hesitate.

– There isn't, I say. – It's a river.

He shrugs.

– The book could not have lied, he says.

I thought so too. But it did.

Maybe he needs to see it too.

So I bite my tongue maybe this is fair punishment for having cocked up so badly and we head off wheeling our bikes through the forest. We get to the restaurant and I see a family on one of the outdoor tables getting up to go. I stop where I am and watch them leave.

Two girls younger than me and a mum and a dad walking off into a big green four-by-four.

– What are you doing? says Jesus.

– One second, I say. – Their drinks.

They drive off. On their table there are glasses between the plates. Not all of them are empty as far as I can see.

Half-lit by streetlights Jesus takes my handlebars.

– Go on, he says.

I run. Through the windows there is a waitress with her back to me. Organising salt or something. Out here the kids had chicken nuggets and chips. Someone had lasagne and stubbed out a fag in the bowl. But there are three glasses of Ribena right in front of me on the table.

It is too sweet and needs more water.

It is amazing.

I drink two of the glasses straight down. The family must have paid inside there is no money on the table not even a tip. I stick a handful of cold chips in my mouth and take the third glass and check the waitress and run back to the forest edge where Jesus is grinning.

– Here, I say. I hold out the glass.

He shakes his head.

– You have it, he says.

I wave it at him but he won't. So I down it too and it is gorgeous and lukewarm and I leave the glass propped up on a root. We walk the bikes out across the car park to the road. There are more cars now than during the day but we find a gap and throw our bikes over the railing.

It is proper night now and the moon is a big crescent and the orange lights of Preston are behind us. I know we should be turning back or even cycling but it is nice to walk in the cool air. And soon the Ribble spreads before us and the country beyond it all weird and flat like the trailer of a spooky Netflix series.

– It was here, I say. – I mean it was supposed to be here. The place where we could cross the river. But it isn't.

Jesus just stares across the flat world.

– Can you smell the sea? he says.

I shrug.

– Come on, he says. – Let's go this way.

Then he gets on his bike and starts cycling away from Preston and I am, – What?

I mean there is no point. There is nothing but sea down there and we need a bridge. I know my map was wrong but if I am honest it never showed a bridge I just thought it would be here. But now he is cycling along the river crazy fast and I head off after him.

– Jesus! I say. – Jesus!

But he is like a mad thing it is all I can do to catch up. My butt still hurts in the seat but my legs are used to it and the mud is hard enough to support my wheels if I keep my distance from the water.

There is nothing on either side of us now not even sheep in the fields no roads or streetlights and it is amazing how much you can see in a crescent moon. I can nearly make out the green of the grass. There is a colder breeze from the sea and Jesus is right you can smell the seaweed the deep fishy rot of it but this is stupid.

– Jesus! Hold up.

But he doesn't and I should be raging but instead I laugh and pedal faster until the night flushes on past me. There is a heron in the distance and I shout, – Fuck off heron, and it flies and I laugh again. The whole world around us is rushing and then the horizon grows wider and Jesus has stopped and I pull up to him.

– You are, I say. – You are a crazy bastard.

He smiles at me. Then he nods at the river.

– It looks flat from here doesn't it?

It is flat.

– Water's always flat, I say.

He nods.

– Water's always flat, he says.

I think he is smiling. Then he turns and cycles away from the river. The grassy soil is dry out here but I don't follow him out as this is getting stupid and we need to head back. But then he turns around and I work out what he is doing.

– You'll fall in! I shout.

But then he starts pedalling towards me. As fast as he can. He is pummelling his big long legs on the bike. He looks like a clown from a kid's show bent low over the handlebars his legs too long his straggly hair and the stupid cape flying off his back. But then he swishes past me and oh God he is over the mud on the river and the water splashes up either side and I am sure he will sink but the bike keeps going and big curtains of water spread like wings after him and then he is across on the other bank on the grass turning to stop and wave at me.

I am laughing so much I can hardly breathe.

– How? I shout as I try to right myself. – How. I mean. How. Is it alright?

– You just need a good run up, he shouts back.

The moon is bright and this is stupid because the water is a river but it must be shallow enough because he made it across. But still I am not sure so I cycle away to get a good run up. I am grinning as I pummel the pedals harder and harder towards the river sure my front wheel is going to dip so I close my eyes and the front wheel sends a steady spray right in my face and I lower my head and I am going to fall and then the front handlebars go and I brake and skid sideways and I do fall but I fall on ground not water and I hurt my side but I look up and Jesus is down the river but I am on his side now and he runs up to me and looks down and I am laughing and he is laughing too.

– I am the Son of God, he says.

30

We sit looking out across the bay. I keep trying to work out how we did it. You can see our bike tracks on the muddy edges of the river. They disappear in the middle. But it must be shallow enough to cycle across because we just did.

I can't believe we made it. I can't stop laughing.

My leggings are utterly soaked and the boggy grass is soaking into my butt but I don't want to move yet. The laughing sets off my coughing and that sets off my breathing but I feel too crazy to let it bug me.

– What else, I say. – What else can you do?

– What do you mean? says Jesus.

– All the miracles, I say. – The magic. Magic of God. Like feeding the five thousand.

Jesus folds his hands.

– Are you hungry?

I shake my head.

– Let me know if you are hungry, he says. – I won't let you hunger while you travel in my presence.

Actually I am hungry. I get my bag off my shoulder and

dig out a chicken wrap. It is all squished but still dry in its wrapper. I offer him one.

He shakes his head and laughs.

– You know the chicken in those was killed too right? And if I took a goose and plucked and cooked it it would taste the same.

I shrug.

– No but what else?

He rubs his face and looks out over the water.

– I can lead you to the truth Orla. I can lead you to a life free of sin. I can offer you forgiveness. Not just for the stealing but for everything. I can open the word of God to you and open your soul to the kingdom of heaven with my Father.

He stares off and I chew for a while.

Then I'm like, – Yeah but people know the word of God. They can read it in the Bible and then do it or like not do it or whatever.

Jesus looks at me and his smile fades.

– I know they can but they don't.

I nod.

– So what else can you do?

I swallow down a bit of wrap the wrong way and it gets stuck in my throat. I start coughing again and get it up but do that slight vomit in the back of my throat and spit out some of the sandwich. Jesus passes over the last of the Dr Pepper and I sip just enough to wet my mouth.

– I could cure your breathing, he says.

I look down and I see his hand palm up to me.

– Don't you touch me, I say.

He withdraws it.

– I won't, he says.

I get out my inhaler not because I need it but to make a point and suck in two big gasps. We will get cold if we sit here long and I have only a vague idea of where to go now. We need to find the smaller river – the River Douglas it's called – that will lead us to Liverpool.

There is some orange sky away from the Ribble.

– Come on, I say standing up. – I need to walk myself dry.

But Jesus stays sat. His arms folded across his knees.

– I rose from the dead Orla.

If he wasn't a grown man I would say he was huffing.

– I swam the abyss and was not drowned, he says. – I can raise the dead to life and I am coming to raise your mother from the dead. You should think of this Orla. Pity those who never witness such as this. I am the Son of God.

I stand looking at him.

– I know you are, I say.

He stares at me sitting on the ground.

– And I am glad you are coming.

It takes him a minute. But eventually he nods. I have my bike ready and I rustle my bag while he stands and wraps his blanket on and gets his stuff together and we wheel the bikes away from the Ribble over the marshy ground.

And I guess he is right. We are going to raise Mum.

I should think about it.

I mean I don't want to. But I can't avoid it now. Like. I should.

Not just digging her up.

What she'll actually say when she is up.

What I'll say.

Love love love.

Blah blah blah.

Why did you have to die?

Like. Like why now?

Why did you leave me alone?

To take care of everyone?

She will be so mad with me.

It gets too big to think about.

So I am glad when we see a light on the horizon.

A building.

– There, I say. – We should head for that.

He doesn't answer.

It takes us ages pushing the bikes over the soggy dips and streams.

But the ground is so bumpy at least I can distract myself by concentrating on the ditches.

My wet leggings.

Streams. Sheep. Silence.

Eventually there is a path that seems to head to the building. And you can smell faint smells of smoke and booze and hear little peeps of conversation and a soft roar of music enough to work out the building must be a pub.

It is bright and noisy when we get close enough to read the sign. The Dolphin Arms. A proper pub on a road with street-lights and everything. It has to be on the map.

So I take off my bike light and hide behind a hedge and get out the book. It seems we are the wrong side of the River Douglas. But there should be a dirt path in a field near here and that would take us to the weir and then we would be back on the path.

At least if I can still trust the book.

– Jesus, I say.

He is staring at the pub. The car park is full so there must be loads of drunk drivers. Music is blasting from the doors and there are smokers on the stairs.

– Jesus, I whisper. – Look I have found a way.

He keeps staring off so I nudge him and show him the book. He looks down and nods.

– I am the Son of God, he says.

– I know you are, I say.

I get on my bike.

– Come on. We have to go this way.

31

We follow the path through another field where the sheep wander without fences. I wonder how they don't go onto the road and get run over. But we get faster cycling now we're off the boggy land and after a while we see a small river and I am pretty sure it is the River Douglas and then after a bit we come to a rickety footbridge.

– Come on slowpoke, I call back.

Jesus nods at me as he squeezes past.

Soon enough we pass a housing estate I reckon Tarleton and it is not long before we find the Tarleton Marina and there are weirs and lights and now I think the book is right again because I can make out the bigger bridges down the river.

So we are on the right track.

Jesus is still cycling ahead but I am thinking that rather than just having a mad panic at dawn we could stop in a forest just out of Tarleton. We have to go that way anyway and we should still be able to get to Liverpool tomorrow night. So when I catch up with him at the bridge I say, – Come on let's find a camp in the forest.

– What?

– There is a forest down here, I say. – We have to go on the main road for a bit but it takes us right past. We should sleep there.

The main road is lit but dead at this time of night and we cross a big car bridge and the world feels empty. The forest comes up on our right and then we come to a big metal gate. I get off and drop my bike with a clung.

– It must be a mansion, I say.

If it is a mansion I can't see any security cameras. The gate is tall but only a low brick wall on either side so it is easy for us to climb over and lift the bikes and then walk through the trees. Avoiding the driveway in the woods. It is dark but we have streetlights behind and bike lights in front. I get scratched by brambles on my face but it is just one more scratch.

This forest is knottier than the one from last night and harder to push through but probably better for avoiding people as long as the mansion guys don't find us. Or have like dogs. Jesus is a good bit ahead just tearing downhill through the brambles and I follow but then he calls to me.

– Orla.

I catch up with him near the riverbank.

He has found an old boarded-up caravan.

Wood across the windows.

The door is held shut with a bit of blue rope.

– Someone might live here, I say.

Jesus touches the door and it creaks open.

– It looks empty, says Jesus.

Breaking and entering is mad exciting. Me and Jamie once got into a caravan in year eight and found a bag of weed but chickened out and threw it in the canal. But even though we thought a dealer was after us for weeks it was a total buzz. But this is different we actually need somewhere to sleep. And there are beds in there but it is weird to be going somewhere with a bed with a man. Of course I have thought of breaking and entering with Jamie or some other guy and like doing it or whatever. But I would never do that with Jesus he is so old and needs a wash and now I do not want to go in at all.

But I can't say any of that.

So I say, – I thought you said we cannot steal?

Jesus just tugs at the blue rope. It is hanging loose.

– The door is open, he says.

He takes off his bike light and carries it in.

I don't want to go in.

But I am too curious.

So I do.

The steps are eaten by rust and the floor creaks and it is dark. There are spiders everywhere and the place stinks of cardboard but it is empty and dry. Jesus flicks the torch over the counters. Old HP bottles and Brown Lemonade whatever that is and at the back a sofa bed and there is the toilet and God it is utter mank and a foldaway table and another door.

We are too close and I can smell Jesus.

– We should sleep here, he says.

But I am like obviously not sharing with him and I move past but my leg brushes his butt and then I shove him and trip out the door and stand at my bike.

I am not sleeping anywhere near him now.

There is a bang and a soft crash and then he is at the door.

– I have found the other bedroom, he says. – I will take that.

I feel the red rising up my neck.

– You take the main room, he says.

I am raging like what did he expect yes he better take the other room but then he is gone.

The sky is beginning to get brighter. It makes the trees look longer and bony. And I really need to go to the toilet but Jesus might be listening.

I wish he would snore. I would know he was asleep.

Then my bike light fades out.

I hit it twice.

Take out the batteries and put them in again.

Dead.

I stand and watch the river.

Mist rises off it.

I really need to go but I can't until Jesus is asleep. But when it is bright enough to see the colour of the leaves I go behind a bush and it feels brilliant and only then can I creep into the caravan. Jesus's door is closed so I lie face down on the sofa bed and fall straight asleep.

32

I wake and the half-light drifts through the boards on the windows.

The bed is so much more comfortable than the boat last night. Never mind it is a sofa. Never mind the spider webs and the smell of paper. The air is too warm but there is a draft from the door and at least you get some shade in here.

Of course Jesus didn't do anything.

I mean I knew he wouldn't. His door is still shut.

There is stuff that needs planned but without a phone I have no way to get ferry timetables or Irish bus routes. There is nothing to do but smell the horrible stink of my armpits.

It is weird how empty my mind goes.

I don't just lie there all day. At some point I get up to pee and I am looking forward to going indoors but the toilet bowl is nothing but cobwebs and blue chemical shit and after looking five times I go outside. At least I can get a bit of wind about me.

I spend a few minutes looking for a USB port for Jesus's bike light but that's dumb as none of the actual lights work in the caravan and there are no batteries for mine either.

I am dying of thirst so I find Jesus's bag and down the last lukewarm smidgeon of Dr Pepper but I am still thirsty. So I go rifling in the cupboards. There are dry lasagne sheets and four tins of tuna but mostly pots and plates and odd-shaped cutlery. So my best choice ends up being four bottles of ancient mineral water on the counter or the sad-looking Brown Lemonade.

The water has floaters in it so Brown Lemonade it is.

It is too warm.

But it has not lost its fizz and it's pretty good.

I never thought I would say it but I cannot bear the idea of another chicken wrap. The last one at the bottom of my bag looks like a bloody smear. Like some animal was stomped in clingfilm. So I end up chucking it out the door as I don't want it near me.

But there are tins of tuna.

So I start looking for a tin opener.

They don't have a turny-handle one so I rattle drawer after drawer and eventually I have this weird claw thing and a long cut on my thumb but the first tin is open.

I drink the brine. It is salty like cold soup but good good good.

I feel my headache wash away as I drink it.

I think it's the salt.

I pick out the chunks with my finger and thumb then do one other tin as well washed down with Brown Lemonade. I could do all four but I should leave some for Jesus.

After that there is nothing to do. There are books – green ones and brown ones and blue hardbacks. There are old magazines – *National Geographic* and *Woman's Own* – and I flick through them. There are some good pictures. The pages are crackly.

Board games. Cluedo. Monopoly.

A set of coloured pencils and paper.

A box of fishhooks with a pharaoh's head on it.

So I look at our clothes. We need to look normal for the ferry. I still have a clean strappy top and my hoody is actually fairly decent. But Jesus will need a clean T-shirt. So I dig one out and find fairy liquid in a cupboard and rub it in then head out to the gravelly riverbank.

I can see the bridge from here.

I take off my shoes and step in.

Rinse my pits with my hands.

It would be lovely to swim.

But if anyone saw a girl swimming in her bra and knickers they would call the cops. So instead I slosh Jesus's T-shirt about in the water with a stick and leave it drying on his handlebars outside the caravan.

And there's still nothing to do.

I could try to sleep but it is too warm. So I pick up the colouring pencils and doodle. I write *Fuck you* and then *Fuck Lemons* and then *Fuck everything* and then scribble it out and start a new page.

Just do spirals.

Fill in the spirals.

I try a skull but I can't get the eyes right. Mrs Lambert says the eyes are level with the ears. That always feels too low in my mind but actually looks better on the page.

I find myself doing Mum.

Her eyes look stupid and I keep rubbing them out. The

mouth is hard and I can't do noses anyway. But actually after a while I get the eyes good. They are shaped like almonds and I do a thousand little brown lines around the pupil. Her hair is not bad either - not the wig at the end but her ponytail and fringe. It's the colour I get right – the mix of brown and yellow and black. Mousy hair. Hazel.

I wonder what hair she will come back with.

Thin cancer hair or the fringe.

I mean she could cut it.

As long as Jesus came with her to the hairdresser.

And the hairdresser was happy to open at night so she wouldn't burn on the grass.

At some point I get sick of the whole thing. I mean what is the point of a picture? But I don't scrunch it up. I just turn away and lie on the seat and leave my hand resting on the page.

I must have fallen asleep.

Because when I wake it is dark. Really dark.

– Jesus?

His door is open.

– Jesus?

There is no one else in the caravan.

Outside his bike is gone.

My heart pops. I rush back in and fall and cut my knee on the step and curse and hop to the table.

There is a note.

He has written something on a page with coloured pencils. The writing is big but my bike light is dead so I limp through the trees to get near the streetlights.

GONE TO DOLPHIN ARMS. BACK BEFORE DAWN.

Fuck.

33

I have no idea how long he has been gone and maybe if he stops I can catch him but he is like a train with those stupid long legs. But there is nothing left to do as he is going to cock this up so I grab my hoody and work the bike through the trees and pedal as fast as I can back past Tarleton with no bloody working bike light.

The village lights fly past behind the trees.

The Dolphin fucking Arms.

Dolphins don't even have arms.

I don't know what the fuck he thought would happen but I am sure it is not going to happen tonight. If he turns up in the blanket he will be in the first cop car out of here. For God's sake he smells like a murderer and that Son of God crap will get him sectioned.

I can just make out the light-grey path but there is the dim glow of streetlights showing where to go and when I get closer to the pub I can hear the chat of smokers outside and up close there are loads of cars in the car park. It might be a wedding?

My heart drops slightly when I see Jesus's bike leant on my side of the hedge.

I look around.

I can't see Jesus.

I don't know what to do.

I am still in my stained gym top. My hoody is nearly passable but I am not like Leila Newman who can get served anywhere she goes. Maybe with a pile of lipstick and the right dress I'd get a pint in some dodgy nightclub but this crowd is older and dressy and I couldn't pass for decent never mind legal.

Never mind I am on the run and can't risk being seen.

I have no clue what to do.

If I leave now I doubt I will see him again.

He is so stupid and just selfish yes fucking selfish.

I'll have to get into the pub.

I creep behind the hedge.

The car park is on my side of the road. Across the way the pub has a big glassy bit with people drinking in it and a smoking bit outside and a kid's playpark and then on the other side there is a cobbled courtyard. The most noise is from the smoking bit and the main glassy building.

The smoking bit is too well-lit so I try the cobbled side.

There are a few cars parked there and a guy in a puffy jacket smoking and shouting on his phone.

The guy doesn't move just keeps shouting at maybe his girlfriend?

When he lights a third fag off the butt of his second I think what the fuck and just put my head down hoody up and walk across the road onto the cobbled bit but go round the back of a Land Rover. He bends to pick up his pint for a second and I see a door and take it and I am in.

It is bright and carpeted and there is a door to the main bar and one to the toilets and I think for a mad second I should go in and wash myself proper but then two women come out of the toilets so I turn quick and push another door on my left and thank God it opens and I find myself in the pub kitchen.

It is really dark.

It is all steel counters. Big steel bins and sinks lit by the FIRE EXIT sign. Everything is humming and shadowy. There are tiles on the walls and what looks like a shutter through to the real bar.

I can hear drinking and chatting through the shutter.

Small chinks of light.

My heart is popping like mad and I usually love the buzz of breaking in but normally there is nothing to lose and here if the cops get me this whole thing will end.

There is a big steel door at the other side but it is locked. There are knives stuck to a magnetic bar on the wall. A drawer of potatoes. A drawer of onions. Two sinks. A salad bar.

The food containers in the salad bar are covered in clingfilm.

I push my fingers through.

The first is coleslaw. The next sweet corn. Then beetroot.

I get myself two big handfuls of coleslaw and it tastes great but goes all down my top. I wash my hands and wipe off my top and then drink loads and loads of water from the tap.

This is madness. I will be caught.

None of this is helping.

So I go right up to the wooden shutters and push them up a bit and I have small lines of light into the crowd.

There are fat men who could be my dad's age. Some people are in fancy dress – flares and sunglasses and spangly clothes. One guy has a green afro wig. There is a table of grannies in matching red tops and Union Jack bunting. There is a space for a band set up at the back.

Everyone looks so old.

There is a banner across the front of the stage. *The Beatless*.

Like the Beatles but with two esses.

There are songs blasting out of the walls but no one on stage. A great big bald guy is tugging a speaker.

Then I see Jesus.

Thank God he had the sense to use the washed T-shirt. It is green and frayed at the neck but miles better than his blanket.

But it is the weirdest thing he is sat at a table and some guys are talking to him. One meaty guy one bald guy and one in glasses and others with their backs to me and Jesus is just leaning across the table nodding his head like he is listening.

But nobody is jumping at him. And I know he stinks like a wet fox but the other fellas at his table are just chatting and drinking beer. Nobody is standing up or kicking off.

Jesus says something.

There is laughter from the other fellas.

He laughs too.

I didn't know he was funny.

And I have no way to hear what they are saying. I think maybe it will all be okay and I am jealous. I had Jesus and now he is talking to other people what about my mother? But I do not think he would leave me forever.

I mean he could.

One of the guys at Jesus's table gets up and waves his pint in a half circle. Then he sits down again.

I wish I could hear what they were saying.

But I can't get all the stupid old people in the pub to shut up and I can't join them so I grab a mug that says BEST AUNT EVER off a shelf and fill it with coleslaw and eat it with my fingers as I stare through the gaps in the shutter.

34

This is what happens.

The guys Jesus is talking to eventually get on stage. The one with glasses is on guitar and there are three more and they sing a bunch of songs. One called *Mean Mr Mustard* and one called *Get Back to Where You Once Belonged* and lots of yeah yeah yeahs. I know some of them from Dad. And the people in the pub love it. A few women get up to dance and there is clapping and whooping.

The whole time I am watching Jesus but he is just watching the band. Drinking from a glass I think beer. Maybe he gets a few odd looks but he does nothing stupid.

The band sings their last song and one of them says, – We'll be back after a ten-minute break folks, and they go back to their table.

Jesus leans over and talks to them.

I think the meaty one shrugs.

Then Jesus walks up to the stage.

By now the rest of the pub is noisy again. The radio has been turned up and the dancers have gone to the bar and there is chatting.

Jesus leans in to the mic.

– Brothers and sisters, he says. – Brothers and sisters I pray a moment of your time.

The barman glances at the meaty band fella and he shrugs. The music is turned down and Jesus starts again.

– Brothers and sisters, he says.

– Fuck off and get a haircut, someone shouts. There is laughter.

– Fuck off back to Somalia, shouts someone else.

There is more laughter. Jesus laughs too. People see him laughing and the talk dies down.

For a second I think this will be alright.

– You are right brother. I do come from a long way away. But I have been talking about life in this country tonight with my friends Michael Jack Seamus and Brian.

He gestures down to the band. The bandmembers wave their pints over their heads. There is a round of applause.

– And Michael Jack Seamus Brian told me of your lives. The pain you live in daily.

He pauses.

– Money shortages. The prisons built for the aged under the name of refuge. How you cannot warm your homes in winter. People you love die isolated in institutions. I know your pain. I know it and I feel it.

He has a good voice. People listen. When he says, – I know your pain, a woman near the shutters opens her hands like she's about to clap.

– But pain can stop. We can end it now. All suffering. Now.

– Is this a Brexit thing? somebody shouts.

There is a murmur from the bar. One table near the shutters turns back to their drinks. The chat gets louder but Jesus doesn't stop.

– And the way through pain yes the only way through pain is kindness. Kindness is all there is. Kindness is all there is. To family of course but beyond the family too. You can end pain – all pain all of it – with kindness.

He pauses. I see a woman next to me checking her watch. The rest of her table are all talking now.

– Kindness is easy. Kindness is opening. Opening to those shaken by hunger by cold by war by old age. To strangers in our streets our shores our cities.

But the jibber jabber starts rising now. Everybody is talking and now one or two people start getting arsey.

Some guy shouts, – Put the tunes on Eddie.

He is losing the crowd.

One table starts chanting, – More songs! More songs!

The barman waves to the meaty fella from the band and there is shrugging and neck-chopping gestures. A man with a white moustache at the bar starts actually barking.

– Kindness is opening our homes to those with none, says Jesus. – Opening our land to those adrift on unsteady rafts with no land of their own and the cold ocean beneath them. Opening the prisons we build for our fathers and mothers and ourselves. Yes even opening our arms. We ache we ache we are all lost but we –

I see the bartender shrug and flip something and the music blasts on and suddenly I can't hear Jesus. He is on stage staring at the mic in his hands.

A small cheer goes up. Jesus taps the mic but the band guy with glasses goes for it and it becomes a tug of war but the meaty guy comes behind and grabs Jesus not exactly wrestling more like hugging him off the stage and Jesus pulls against him but gets dragged to his seat.

The music blares.

The table near me are chatting loudly. I hear the word *Somalian*.

I can't see Jesus through the crowd.

I feel sick and I just want to go.

But then the music dies down and the glasses guy from the band switches on the mic.

– Sorry about my friend, he says. – I think it is safe to say we all just came here to have a good time!

A slight cheer goes up again.

– No hard feelings my foreign friend eh?

The rest of the band is setting up around him and the crowd parts. I see Jesus sat at the table his head down. I think he is crying. The moustached barking man is near the door and the audience claps again.

– No hard feelings mate. But now –

Then Jesus starts singing.

I wonder how his voice can be so loud. I can hear him singing over the mic and over all the chat. His voice silences the whole bar and everyone puts their glasses down and watches.

His voice is pure and lovely. He sings one long slow note and I can feel it shaking in my body from the ground up through my lungs to the tips of my hair. It is a long slow sound that feels like breath on my cheek halfway between a child crying and an ox braying and I want to cry and laugh. I swear it is my mother's breath and my eyes start to ache with the pressure of tears and I feel guilty so guilty for all I have done and even though I will do it again I am sore in my ribs for the wrong I do in my gut and yet I know I can make it better and I would follow Jesus anywhere he tells me to.

I want to say sorry to Dad.

Sorry to Jamie.

My whole body is shaking.

Then I see the glasses guy come over. He has a guitar case in his hands and he rams it hard into the side of Jesus's face. Jesus falls off the chair and the sound stops.

There is a moment's silence.

I shake like I am freezing.

I look around as other people blink.

Some of them have tears on their faces.

Then someone cheers.

– Get him out of here, shouts someone else.

Men step between Jesus and the shutters. I cannot see him anymore. All I can hear is the barking man and glasses chinking and I think I see Jesus lifted out towards the far door then the drummer hits his sticks together and says, – One, two, one, two, three, four! and they are singing *Help I Need Somebody* and there is applause and two women head to the dance floor and I grab a big sharp knife from the metallic bar on the wall and run out of the pub the way I came in.

35

I am on the cobbled bit outside the pub but it is all kicking off on the far side of the building and there is a crowd at the corner but I can't see Jesus. I am in a total panic behind a car but then I see a woman coming over to me.

– Alright love are you okay?

She is in a blue spangly dress maybe fortyish smoking and texting beside me. It's just her and me on the cobbled bit.

– You shouldn't be out here at this time of night love.

She stubs out her fag and puts her phone in her bag and comes over and I should run but I can't see Jesus and she hunkers down to me.

– Look at the state of you, she says. – Where is your mother?

Booze. Perfume. But I am backing off and I need to see where the fuck Jesus is and I am looking over her hair and I try to pull away but now the woman has me by the shoulders.

– Just fuck off, I say. – Please just fuck off.

– Love be chill, she says. – Calm down. Just calm down a second.

But she is holding me trying to I don't know what but she should stop holding me and then I see Jesus in the car park pushing against two big bouncers and one of them shoves him but Jesus comes back and the bouncer decks him and he drops and this woman should stop fucking holding me so I shake and lift the knife and she screams.

– You stabbed me!

There is a tiny cut on her finger!

– There is a tiny cut on your finger!

But she runs into the pub. And it is going from bad to worse but I see Jesus pushing into the bouncers again so I run across the road and in the car park there are two people no three people around him the two big guys in bouncer jackets and the white-haired barking guy. One of the bouncers shouts, – Stop getting up, and shoves Jesus hard on his ass again and his head whacks the ground.

But he gets back up staggering into them.

There is blood all down his front.

The old guy is still shouting gobbledegook. The bouncers are talking low. I sneak behind the cars to get closer.

Jesus's eyes and face are all blood on one side. I can't fully see from here. His voice is fucked I can only make out some words like, – Father, and, – Love, but all slurry.

One of the big guys says, – Just stay down, and decks Jesus again on the side of the head.

He falls and I feel it.

– Stop it!

I am running out of the bushes. I am bloody stupid and I may as well just give everything up they will see my face but I don't know what to do. So I run up shouting, – I'll call the cops! I will call the cops I fucking swear if you lay a hand on him even a single finger!

The men turn their big backs like wardrobe doors but I push past and there is Jesus and his face is mushy and I can only see one eye. I run up and grab him and I just hold him from behind his head on my chest and I am screaming and waving the knife and my words make no sense so I stop.

There is a moment of silence as they watch me.

– Darling, says one bouncer. – Where did you get that knife?

– Just fuck off and stop battering him!

Jesus struggles against my arm. – No, he says. – No Orla you don't ubblestand.

He tries to stand but slips on his ass and I hold his head tight.

– Do you know this man? says the other bouncer crouching.

– Fuck them John. They must be gypsies, says the first guy.

He starts walking away. Then over by the pub I see the woman who grabbed me. She is outside the back door with a big dramatic white cloth held to her hand and there is a man with her in a leather jacket and she is pointing at me.

There are too many people now. Bouncers and the woman and the barking fella. They can all see my face and Jesus's face.

– Is this guy grooming you? says the crouching bouncer.

– Just fuck off you fucking dickbag! I scream.

The moustached fella starts laughing. He is old and in a suit and I can smell the booze on him from here.

– Fuck them John, says the first bouncer. – They are in cahoots.

I cannot stand being seen by them all and so I tug Jesus to a gap in the fence waving the knife. I have never got this close to him he is bony and light as a bird and I think he is crying but I have to get out of here. And I know our bikes are on the other side of the car park but I cannot risk giving them away so I just drag him down the marshy field. The woman holding her cut finger like a fucking newborn is talking to the bouncer and they might come after us so I try to make as much distance as I can. The ground is all mud and one of Jesus's legs doesn't seem to work and the moon is gone. It is dark but I know the river is up this way and I can circle back for the bikes once I have kicked Jesus's arse for being so stupid I mean stupid. So I drag him and he has given up resisting just leaning on me but there are small half-words under his breath and then I hear a wet knock and he drops to the ground and I see a rock fall in front of us.

– Fuck off back to Pakistan you fucking gypsy bastards.

Jesus falls holding his face and I turn to see the moustached guy following us in the last glimmer of the streetlights.

I pick up the rock and throw it at him.

– I'll knife you! I will bloody stab you!

He laughs and hops back towards the road. I throw the knife after him and it goes skitting through the grass. Then I grab Jesus and half carry half drag him away through silent sheep munching in the darkness until the ground gets smooshier underfoot and streams run through the soil. In the distance I can see the blue lights of a cop car and I feel my breath tickle but there is no time for that now I don't lose it I can't I just jerk Jesus forward like a crap partner in a three-legged race. I curse at him, – Fuck, I say, – Get up you stupid crying baby, but he just makes small breathy noises. We are off across the moors hop-walking like twenty minutes more him leaning on me until he is just too heavy and awkward and I drop-push him into a muddy ditch by a stream and I get down and face him.

36

There is a light rain now. It is so bloody dark. I can see the shape of his head but can't see the difference between blood and beard even though I am right up near him. He is breathing small shivery breaths like Lily when she falls asleep crying and whispering some words in like French or Bible language I don't know.

– Why did you leave me? I say.

He does not speak. Just lies slumped against the muddy bank. But I know he is awake. I was just carrying him and his feet were moving and he is bloody awake.

– Why did you leave me? I say again. And I take off my hoody even though it is raining and I am sure I have got his blood all down it now. And I wind the sleeve around my fist and I think about whacking him in the face and I say a third time, – Why did you go?

– I am the Son of God, he says.

I get up and I do not shout he is battered enough but I do not know what to do. There is a stream and everything is wet already but I put the sleeve of my hoody in the stream. I don't know why. But the only thing that makes sense is I go to Jesus and even though I can't see well enough I wipe his head with the wet sleeve.

There's no way I can wear it on the ferry now.

– You think they want to hear about you? I say to him. – Why the hell would they want to hear about you?

I think he is crying. He takes the sleeve and holds the hoody into his face leaving me to soak bare armed in the drizzle.

– Why are you crying for? I say. – What is the point in that?

He goes on weeping and I am getting angrier and angrier. What in the hell is the point of a grown man crying? I feel my fists going in and out. I want to pull the hoody away and leave him like the useless big shit he is.

He lifts his head.

– Don't you understand Orla? he says. – I have to make them see. I have to make them see or they will be lost. So many have been lost Orla. Who will lead them back if not the shepherd?

– No, I shout.

I stand up.

I can feel my breathing going. I have kept it at bay but I cannot keep it at bay forever.

– No that is not right. You said you would help me. You said you would. You said you would come to Ireland and you can't just leave me in the woods.

Jesus sniffles.

– I was coming back to you. What matters –

– No, I say again. – You can't just leave me. I am fourteen years old. I could have been killed or murdered and you cannot abandon me in the middle of the woods at night it is not right.

Jesus goes quiet. Weeping.

I wish I could see his face.

– I am the Son of God, he says.

I reach down and yank my hoody from him.

– Give me my hoody, I shout. – I am getting wet here.

I put it on and screw the blood.

– I am the Son of –

I scream.

– You are not the Son of God, I shout. – You are some bloody vampire that is all you are. You don't die and you have magic blood and make other things drink your blood to come back to life and you burn in the sun and the only thing that does that is vampires and I do not want you sucking on me any longer.

And I run. And it is dark and I have water in my eyes and I trip in a small stream and lose my shoe and at first I can't find it but then I do and sit to put it on and run run run but my breath goes bad and I have to stop. And I know Dad would be shouting at me for getting so wet and would have me in the car waving a bloody inhaler in my face but I don't even have my inhaler it must be in the caravan and I am totally covered in mud.

But I make it back to the road wheezing the whole way and the angle I go is wrong so it takes me proper ages out at the wrong part of the road and I wake a sheep that has found its way onto the tarmac and I get soaked through to my pants. But when I find my way back to the Dolphin fucking Arms the pub is dark and closed and the car park is empty in the rainy streetlights.

I am really shivery and breathy.

My hair is stuck down my face and every time the hoody touches my back I shake and cough.

When I get to the bikes I take Jesus's bike light off and wheel his bike into a ditch like I am ditching stolen goods.

I mean I am ditching stolen goods.

Then I hop on my bike and make my way back to the canal and try to calm my breath. It kind of works but my mouth keeps filling with water running off my face making me splutter. The river is nearly invisible through the rain.

The ground just one massive puddle it is slow going.

But by the time I get to the rickety footbridge the rain is stopped.

Through the clouds the sky is grey rather than black.

I guess dawn is coming.

And yes I cried I cried the whole way of course and now my throat is raw from coughing and my body is shaky.

But I know I can't go.

I can't cycle to the caravan and fall asleep in the dry room.

I have left Jesus battered in a ditch.

With no protection from the sun.

I have to go back.

So after a while of standing there trying to find an excuse I do. I turn back.

When I get to the field he is easy to find. It is getting brighter but more than that there are dead animals around him. Ducks with ripped-out throats. A baby black sheep with blood in its wool. Loose feathers blowing over the wet grass in handfuls.

He is lying on the soil with no blanket. Flat in the mud like a dead body. His eye is mushy with blood and his beard is a big scab.

The sun is still under the horizon but there is a pink edge to the sky. A faint steam is rising off Jesus's clothes.

I stand over him and shake him.

I slap him and punch him and then just try to drag him.

– Get up, I say. – Get up get up get up.

He does not move.

– You are the Son of God so get up and walk again.

Nothing.

– Move your stupid bloody arse, and I boot him.

Nothing happens.

So I tug him by his bony arm. Drag him on the wet grass past the hump of a dead rabbit.

The Dolphin Arms is too far I will never make it. I am not sure he is breathing but I am sure he cannot walk. There is at most an hour until the sun is fully up and I don't know what will happen then.

I tug him over the edge of a ditch and he slides down into a stream.

I'll not get him out again.

So I stick my hands into the muddy bank and take out a great wet handful of mud and plaster it onto Jesus's chest. And I begin to bury Jesus before the sun comes up.

37

Burying Jesus is very different from burying a normal person. I have to slap handful after handful of mud onto his jeans and arms touching his cold body where sunlight could reach his skin and then an extra layer of protection on his clothes. Give him a blanket of mud. Burying Jesus is less like a funeral and more like burying your mother on the beach caking wet sand on her legs and body until you can only see a head ha ha isn't it magic Mummy is decapitated lol. We used to do that. I would bury her legs and take photos on her phone to show her as a mermaid or a head and then she would do me and I'd get sand under my swimsuit and we'd have to find a warm puddle to get the streaks off our legs.

Burying Mum in real life was nothing like this. It took a week to even get the body to Ireland. She died on Tuesday and we had been waiting for her to die for three weeks since she stopped talking and the nurses asked for someone to stay in the ward every night. Sinead was over from Ireland to help look after Mum and she was always in the house and if not her then Bob or Sue would take turns looking after Lily or driving me to school while Dad hung out in the hospital or sat drinking on the sofa. I wanted to be off school but they said there would be time as the Easter break was coming and she was bound to make it to that but she didn't make it to that.

She died on Tuesday when I was in Science and Lemons was covering for Hanniway. Jamie was texting me horror GIFs with teachers' heads photoshopped on and there was one where Lemons was a woman with gigantic boobs getting stabbed in the boob and I burst out laughing and Lemons saw it and took my phone and gave me detention. Then Sinead came and there was shouting in the corridor and I was taken out of detention and she led me out carrying my bag and I knew Mum was dead then because why would she carry my bag and when we got into the car Dad didn't smell of booze and then I knew for sure.

I didn't get to see her body but I wasn't sure I wanted to. It had gotten so I hated visiting her. When she stopped talking I tried sitting there but there was nothing to say and it made me angry and then bored and then guilty because I was bored and then angry again. But Dad took a photo and showed it to me in the car and she looked like herself only yellower.

Sinead said it was okay to feel however I felt.

Then we went home and it all felt stupid.

We had to bury her in the McGonagle family plot in Drumahoe with her and Sinead's brother and mother as that is what she wanted. So Dad spent the week phoning and losing his temper while Sinead or Bob or Sue tidied or sorted crap out. They didn't have to do much cooking as loads of neighbours even Mrs Arbuckle came over with bowls of lasagne or plates of sandwiches. I didn't have to go to school then but that meant I just sat in the house with everyone coming over feeling sorry for me rubbing their hands. Zoe came over with her mum and then twice on her own. Sue took me out to get my hair done and buy a dress for the funeral. I met Claire for the first full hour session. Mostly I was on my phone.

Jamie kept texting and it was Monday the day before we were flying to Ireland when he sent me a photo of his airgun. I was going mad with Sue packing my bag and I didn't say anything to Sue or Dad just cycled out and Jamie was like, – Let's get Lemons's car. So everyone else was in school and us outside the fence taking shots at his tyres. I missed every time. Jamie got it a bunch. He put two holes in the mirror and a bunch of cracks in the back window but we couldn't pop the tyres. I laughed like mad and kept feeling guilty for laughing but then he would pop another shot. Then we saw Hargreaves walking out the back door and panicked and ran and although they never could say it was Jamie for sure they have been on his back ever since. But I came home buzzing and the bags were packed and I cried that night in bed with Sinead rubbing my back and Dad was sober and they got me up and we sat eating Weetabix and chatted about Mum and how things might change. That was okay.

Ireland was great. I mean I feel bad saying it but it was. Sinead and Majella and Barry all the cousins were constantly buzzing around and sometimes they cried too but most of the time not and we all knew that we all knew Mum. I kept feeling guilty for enjoying the attention but then someone would hug me or give me a fiver and we sat up late talking and joking. Everyone kept saying it was a pity we couldn't have a real wake but I have never been to a wake. I just know that I was not on my own but instead of getting mad I liked them around. There were photos of Mum everywhere. I slept with Cathy-Anne in the bottom bunk with Dad in the top and I heard him crying at night but at least he was sober.

Sunny at the funeral. Easter Wednesday. The priest talked about rebirth. I didn't recognise most people but Sinead took my hand and said, – Your mammy would be so proud of you, and she cried and I cried and Lily hugged me and said it would all be okay and we laughed and that was alright too.

We stayed longer than the school holidays. We did bowling and swimming and the cinema. I got new trainers. When we had to pack we had one entire suitcase full of Easter eggs.

Then we came back and it was just me and Dad and Lily.

And people stopped visiting and we had to give the casserole dishes back and I was told I could have another few days off school but that meant sitting looking at Dad itching to day-drink or taking Lily to the park when I knew he would be opening a few sneaky cans at home. He got me a bunch of sessions with Claire. But the house was empty and there was no life and I couldn't sit anymore. So I went back to school the day after Jamie got done for the phones and Dad was drinking every night and we went to mass and he called Father Michael an obsequious prick. And apart from that everything was so fucking normal as if we should just all get on with things and that was that.

All of which is so different from burying Jesus. I never saw Mum's body. Here I have to plaster him carefully with mud. I dig out a shallow hole to rest his head in and use the mud to coat his arms and wrap him in a wet slimy layer. I don't coat his face with mud in case he needs to breathe but I wrap his head with my hoody. I cake his ankles where they stick out the bottom of Dad's jeans. I try to cover the rest of him as best I can building a body-shaped hump in the ditch. A giant holy mud pie. The sun starts popping over the horizon and steam starts to rise from the hump leaving a faint smell of barbeque in the drizzle. So where I see the steam rise I work my fingers sore. Drop a big pile on his crotch and pat it with my forearm. Plaster handful after handful on his chest. Sometimes rubbing the clattered fringe off my face with the cleanest part of my arm when the tears get tickly on my nose. Sometimes scraping big handfuls off the bed of the stream and patting him down like let's play Mummy's-Just-a-Head on Morecambe beach tra-la-la tra-la-lee tra-la-la lay-dee-o.

38

The sun is up but where the river feeds the bay the sky is still dark. I am totally clattered up my arms all over my top and down my leggings. My hair is mudcake. I am cold inside my body and so shivery I don't think I could sleep. But I am done with tears and my breathing is as close as it is going to get to normal and steam has stopped rising off Jesus. I reckon all you would notice is a dirty old hoody in a ditch and a few dead animals.

So I sit on the hump because it's not like my leggings are going to get any dirtier.

It is good to just sit and let my arms hang.

The summer before she died we went camping in Scotland. Glamping I mean a cabin with a kitchen. We had known Mum was dying for months and mostly they gave me space but there was no space in the cabin. And me and Mum had a particularly bad blowout one night. I had started on Dad – he was trying to get us to play Cluedo – and he ended up hid in the bedroom with Lily while me and Mum had it out on the veranda. I called her the c-word and ran off until Dad found me hid on the beach around midnight by the light of my phone and put me to sleep on the sofa bed.

But next morning she woke me it must have been about five. I knew I was in for it after the c-word but she put a juice on the coffee table and waved at me from the door.

– Put on your shoes, she said.

I was, – What?

So we snuck out and she led me down to the beach and there were snails all down the path and we tried not to crunch our feet on them. I thought I was in trouble but it was also like we were kids sneaking out for a midnight feast and I didn't know whether to laugh or run. And when we got to the beach I was shivering and breathy but she put her arms around me looking out at the sea.

– Those are oil rigs, she said pointing at black shapes on the water. – There's probably workers out there on the late shift. And they might be watching us.

I could feel her breath on my cheek. We didn't say anything about the c-word or dying. Just waved a bit to the invisible oilmen who obviously couldn't see us.

Mostly we just stood.

It was nice.

Eventually it got too bright and we got cold and had to climb back up the steps but I helped her put out the cereals and we ate the last croissants ourselves before the others got up and we never mentioned the c-word again.

And yes there were good times loads of them. Christmases. When she was pregnant with Lily and we got a bucket of KFC and tried to finish it before Dad came home and even though I vomited we were still laughing when he came in shaking snow out of his hair with nothing left but a mini corn on the cob and some cold chips. There was a day sandboarding when we laughed and laughed each of us with split lips. Even when Lily was just born Mum let me carry her around the hospital bed because she knew I wasn't as bad as everyone said.

But there was also bad stuff. Like the first time she caught me with lipsticks under my bed and I said they were Zoe's and she knew I was lying. Like when she was called in to the head and I knew she would take his word over mine. She knew I was lifting and at the end she just stopped talking about it. I knew she was ashamed of me lifting. Of me.

When her chin got fat we stopped looking each other in the face. And when Dad gave up work and said he was putting my phone on pay-as-you-go and I went ballistic I found her crying on the toilet. And once when Dad was moving her in the hospital bed I saw her pad and got disgusted. I hated the vomit in her hair. Hated the smell of it.

I don't know if I want Mum to come back in her own body. Even on the beach there were lumps of cancer boiling in her. If Jesus brings her back will it be the skinny woman in Scotland dying inside? The hospital mum with painted-on eyebrows? Or will it be the young mum in a bikini from photos with no stretchmarks?

She wouldn't know what happened.

To her. To us.

Mum always said glamping was too close to nature. And the odd time when we went to mass she always said, – Thank God that's over, and would roll her eyes at me when the priest came to chat to us.

Will she have to be a Holy Joe when she comes back?

Are her choices to travel with Jesus or burn on the grass?

Whatever happens she will die again.

Unless she had a body that could not die. A body of I don't know of light.

Does light not die?

How would that be her?

If there is a heaven of singing and eternal joy I do not know if I want it. Yes happiness forever sounds great. But if all we feel is happiness with no change no talk don't see each other just sing? Eternal joy where I cannot move or change like how will it be her?

How will it be me?

And not some other being that isn't me?

If I really wanted her back it would probably be a time machine. If I could go back before the cancer and hit her with a healing ray. Because it is not fair that she is dead. Zoe's grandad had throat cancer and they cut it out and now he just speaks whispery and watches his food. That. I want that. Some small cancer they can chop out and life goes on. Or better no cancer at all like nearly everyone else's mum. I would hit her with the healing ray and then we could have time.

I mean I know she would still die at some point.

Maybe I could time machine that away too.

I don't know.

The real thing I want is her back. Her. The good bits and the bad bits. Not an unchanging holy ghost of light forever singing. I want her. That bit of her that made toast and got surprised. That could wave at oil-rig workers. Could sit with me on a wet pile of mud covered in dirt and not act the way I thought she would. Do things she never did before. Could be surprised.

39

I may have fallen asleep.

I am not sure.

It is brighter now. I can see insects.

Worms in the soil.

I am glad I was digging in the dark because I would not want to touch them now.

What will happen if they dig into Jesus's body?

Will they live forever?

Will they burn up like incense if they leave his body?

It is not fair.

I don't want other people's mothers to die. I hate Zoe's mum but not even her. But it is not fair that Zoe gets to sit with her talking about piano classes or bloody tennis shoes. Sophie's mum has depression and was in mental health care for a year after losing a baby but Sophie can talk to her sit at the end of her bed and tell her new stuff. Sue's boys have Sue even if she gets a divorce. Even Jamie's mum who never lets me see him and tries to punish him constantly for all the things his brother did. He has her. He can see her.

It's not fair.

All I have are memories.
Good bits and bad bits.
That's all I have.
I don't want to give them up.
But I can't imagine her wanting either of Jesus's choices.
Stay near him forever or go into the light.
I can't.

At some point I get up. I know I do because I am on my bike. I stop and feel my face and it seems I have tried to wash some of the mud off. I guess in the canal because I am beside it and I can see Hesketh across the water. I may have stood there a while and I may have fallen asleep standing up.

A woman walking her dog looks right into my face and does not say anything.

I notice the heat of the sun on my neck.

Then I am in Hesketh and I guess I cycled into town. I reckon if anyone sees me they will call the cops I am so covered in mud. But I am in a phone booth and I have a two-pound coin in my hands.

I don't know where I got the coin.

There is a poster on the wall for the circus and I wonder if it is the same circus that I saw with Zoe and I give a little laugh because there is a picture of an elephant and under that is the name Fantasmo. Fantasmo the saddest elephant in the world. It must be the same circus. I think I remember laughing.

Then I put money in the phone and phone Sinead.

– Sinead, I say when she picks up.

The line is silent.

– Orla? she says.

– Sinead this is Orla, I say.

– Oh my God Orla darling. Where are you? Your dad is going mad trying to find you sweetheart. Please tell us where you are.

– Sinead, I say and my voice is all crotchety. – I was thinking of coming over. To visit you for a while.

– What? Where are you pet? Are you in Ireland?

– I was going to come over. To see you all.

– Orla. Tell me where you are love.

– I might not bother coming now, I say.

There is a pause.

– Orla listen very carefully to me now my darling. Of course you can come over whenever you want. Of course you can we would love to have you but we really need to know where you are right now. Tell me listen to me where are you pet?

I go silent for a bit just looking at the phone.

– I am in a phone box, I say.

– Orla are you with someone? Or are you on your own?

But then I stumble into the thingummy I mean the bit I mean the thing the phone hangs on. Click. She goes off.

No change comes out of the phone.

No wonder people switched to mobiles.

I know I cycled down past the canal. I think I remember asking someone for money. But that might have been before the phone call? I may have tried to get some food but I don't think I managed. But at some point I must have got back to the caravan in the forest because I drank the rest of the Brown Lemonade and passed out on the sofa bed as the sun started to shine hotter and hotter outside.

40

When I wake I am all ache and don't want to move.

Eyeballs and jaw and bones all ache.

My head the worst.

I am so dirty. Hair hard with mud. My fingers like something from *The Walking Dead*. My top doesn't smell of sweat it just smells like mud.

But all I can think of is the phone call.

They will know where I am now. Near Hesketh. All they have to do is trace the call.

But more than that I said I was not coming to Ireland.

So where the hell am I going?

Eventually I need to pee.

I squat outside the caravan and the air is already midgey. I must have slept most of the day. My legs are muddy even through my leggings.

I potter round a bit. Put clothes in bags. Dig out Jesus's bag. *Traffic-Free* bloody *Cycle Paths*. I keep sniffing the mineral water with the floaters and shuddering. When I get the two tins of tuna open and another cut on my thumb I drink the brine and it is better than the meat it is good good good but I am still thirsty.

Like awful I-need-water-now thirsty.

Then it occurs to me there is a bloody river outside that cannot be much worse than floatery water. And I know it must have sewage and *E. coli* in it and Mum would shout at me if I drank river water.

But if I am not going to Ireland then I can do anything I want.

So I walk through the trees. I can see the bridge but the streetlights aren't on yet. I get down on my knees to take a handful to drink but it is so nice on my skin I just kind of stumble in.

My whole body sunk in the cool water.

No one can see me I am sure of it.

I chuck my leggings top knickers all off and dunk my head under.

Take two big drinks. Big drinks of river.

It tastes of gritty dust and it is cold.

The headache fades a bit.

If someone comes I will just scream at them until they go.

I lie on my back and kick away from the edge just let myself bob. The river pulls me and I paddle against it. Kick against another stone until I am under the bridge. Staring up at the underside. The sky.

I let my head sink while I float and try to drink on my back and end up spluttering in the water. Then more floating.

I spend a while shouting under the bridge.

First curses. Then just sounds.

Blow bubbles in the water.

Try to tug my fingers through my hair.

When I climb onto the bank the streetlights have started

to come on and my bones are cold. My fingers are less muddy but I know I could do with a hairbrush. I have no towel but I go to the caravan and dig out the clean clothes and under-wear I was saving for the ferry.

The clean clothes feel good on my wet skin.

And I don't know what I should do. I still have money for ferry tickets. But if I am not going to Ireland I can go any-where. But then it occurs to me that actually I know exactly what I want.

I want a fish supper and a can of Coke.

Or oh my God a cheeseburger.

So I look at our bags. I decide to carry both just in case and it is awkwarder with two. But I wheel my bike through the woods to the little wall and chuck it onto the road. There are a few cars about as I cross the bridge and then I am on the road into Tarleton.

They must have takeaways in Tarleton.

Then an ambulance passes with flashing lights and for a second I think it is cops and it spooks me. Fuck Tarleton. So I head down the cycle path to Hesketh because I think I saw a KFC on Google Maps there once.

My stomach cramps as I go.

But further along the towpath I see something. There is a big field between Tarleton and Hesketh. I have passed it a few times but now it is full of cars. People are parking in it and electric lights are set up.

I can smell popcorn and God it smells amazing.

I reckon this has to be the circus.

Why else would cars be parked in a field?

So I leave my bike and bags in the bush and push my way

through and climb over the fence and I was right a big tent is set in the next field. There are families with kids coming out of cars heading to the big tent and my mouth is watering for popcorn.

Now this is clearly madness there are so many people here who could see me what if one of the clowns recognises me? Or there are cops there?

But then I think this is amazing.

Say worst comes to worst and Sinead phoned Dad and he phoned the cops and the cops traced the call and Hesketh is crawling with cops there is no way they will expect me to be here in the circus. And it is dark no one will see my hair is ratty or notice a kid on her own.

But more than that the popcorn smells amazing and I am going to have some.

There are so many people shoving around and I try to keep my face low but everyone is looking at the lights the balloons the hay. I see the elephant cage but it is empty and I think maybe poor Fantasmo is dead. I queue up behind a family of a dad and mum with two sons with my head down.

The queue takes a while.

I only see the prices when I get near the kiosk: £30 RING-SIDE or £20 MIDDLE or £12.50 BACK ROW. UPGRADE £7.50 FOR DRINK AND POPCORN. I fumble the money. I thought it would be cheaper. But now there are loads of people behind me but if I do this it means I will definitely not have enough for the ferry for both of us and maybe I need a second but then the man is looking at me.

– Just one? he says.

I fumble my bumbag zip.

– I just. Just, and I nearly drop my notes.

– Back row love?

He wags the ticket in front of me.

The people behind are looking.

– Popcorn upgrade, I shout and hand the cash over.

Twenty quid ping there goes the money.

A ferry ticket. A whole new life.

He thrusts a ticket and an upgrade voucher to me. I think my breath is going to go but I follow the crowd to the popcorn and the queue is thinner and a woman in sequins leans over the popcorn cage to me and says, – Sweet or salty or mixed?

I don't know.

– Mixed, I say.

Then I wait and ask for water instead of the Coke she offers and I follow the crowd into the tent where a clown takes my ticket and leads me through the dark to my seat.

I take a big bite of popcorn in my mouth.

It is really really great.

I wait for the show to begin.

41

So I sit through the entire show. Other people are chatting or on their phones but I watch it all. My water is great – less gritty than river – but the popcorn makes my mouth dry. But a woman comes round with ice cream and I keep buying more water.

Two quid a go. A rip-off.

But I nearly let her keep the change I am that thirsty.

The show starts mostly the same as before but no Chinese acrobats. Maybe they have other jobs. But then they get the elephant out this time doing tricks and giving rides in the interval.

It is definitely the same one.

Fantasmo.

She.

He.

I decide she is a female elephant.

She doesn't have a bandage anymore but is all spangles and glitz and is by a mile the best part of the show.

First it's the Scottish ringmaster cracking jokes and a whip, – You may get wet in the front row! then Fantasmo chases him and then there's a mime which is like alright and then Fantasmo lifts the popcorn woman in her trunk and the woman gets on a seesaw and a guy jumps on the other end and springs her onto Fantasmo's back. That's the best bit. After that it's the clowns again throwing fruit around a volunteer and the ticker tape.

I don't laugh like a seal this time but I do still think it is funny.

Then a high-wire woman who is the popcorn woman I think and then a dog guy. Dog guy big deal could have been on *America's Got Talent*. But by this time some of the teenagers are just flat-out talking or heading out the back. So then there is an interval and people get photos with the elephant for a fiver or a short ride for twelve quid.

Head down I go up.

Mainly to buy more water. But also to see Fantasmo up close.

She has these big wrinkly eyes.

But they look tiny in her massive head. Even though they are big for actual eyes.

One of the clowns helps kids onto her back and leads her round and poses with her for photos. He has a short stick and taps Fantasmo behind her knee to get her to stand and puts a hand on her trunk to get her to sit.

She is so slow.

She could crush any of the kids if she wanted.

But actually the jangly elephant necklaces look bloody annoying. I can see where her bandage was before and now there's a sequiny bangle on it.

That would annoy the hell out of me.

The lights go down and it is time to start again. So I take my seat and the place looks emptier. Some people haven't come back. There are even spaces at the front and I move up a couple of seats.

The second half starts with a song from *The Greatest Showman* with a bunch of people dressed up like the movie even the bearded woman but I am pretty sure it is all just the clowns in costumes. Then the ringmaster with magic tricks – flowers and buckets of glitter and the last one is good he changes the popcorn woman's clothes by dropping a Hula-Hoop over her. Then the clowns again doing ladder tricks and lastly two songs with Fantasmo and the dog guy walking around the ring. Then there is clapping and the lights go on and there are more elephant rides and it is over.

The tent is only about a third full at the end.

There are not many kids queuing for Fantasmo now and the clown unbuckles her pretty quickly and leads her out the back as everyone leaves and in a minute I am one of the last people in the tent and they are already moving the seats.

I mean the thing is I get it.

I enjoyed the show I actually did. It is better than riding a stupid bloody bike. But it was also kind of crap. The teenagers who left at the break were not wrong. I can watch better on my phone any time. Like a girl shooting arrows with her toes. A guy hanging off the Eiffel Tower by one arm. All of which makes a girl jumping off an elephant kind of ordinary.

It is a bit sad I reckon.

I mean not sad like dying or getting chucked out of school. So I don't know why I should be moping around when they come to take my chair. I don't even have any hard bits of popcorn left to suck.

– You alright love?

The popcorn woman.

I mumble something and stand up and walk off.

I am not sure where though.

The field car park is emptying. The tent is nearly done with stragglers and soon it will just be me and circus workers.

People used to run away with the circus. Didn't they?

I could do that.

I don't want to do that.

I stand between two trucks and watch the ringmaster muttering to Fantasmo as he walks her to her cage. There is a bale of hay there and a big tub too. I move around the front of a truck so he can't see me.

He doesn't put her in the cage. He just chains a padlock to the harness on her neck and lets her pick at the hay. She pulls big trunkfuls out and folds them up stuffing them in the flap of her mouth.

Then she goes for the tub of water.

Sucks it up and flicks a big scoot over her back.

– Can I help you sweetheart?

It is the ringmaster. He's an old fella and he has seen me. He is keeping his distance stood on the steps of a caravan.

– No I'm fine.

I walk off back to my bike.

The bloody bike.

I can go anywhere.

But I don't want to go anywhere.

I mean there is something I maybe want but it is dumb.

But by the time I am on the bike on the towpath and have shouldered both bags I have a pretty good idea of the really dumb thing I want.

I sit on the saddle listening to the circus ones lift and tidy and chat and drift off to their caravans. Some of the clowns drive away. In normal cars. A small rain blows up across the water making everything damp.

My brain starts ticking.

Every now and then I move my bike a little further so I can see where Fantasmo has wandered on her length of chain.

See I kind of want that elephant.

42

So by the time I am over near the Dolphin Arms my clothes are wet again but I like it after the hot day. But it is hard to see because Jesus's bike light is dull and then stops working altogether.

I get wetter. I have to take it slow on the bumpy ground.

The pub looks shut now so it must be either after midnight or a Sunday. But there are streetlights on and when I get to where I threw Jesus's bike it is gone.

I feel a small pop in my heart.

Maybe he has gone too.

Or maybe someone just stole his bike.

But there is no point worrying until I have checked. The only way to find Jesus is to head from the riverside to the road following every ditch that crosses the field looking out for dead animals. So I cycle to the water and I think this is the way I dragged him.

And I know I am right when I pass a hump that turns out to be a dead lamb.

I walk the bike and see another hump in a ditch and it is Jesus.

Just lying there as the rain fills the stream around him.

It is hard to see what is man and what is mud but I drop the bags and kneel down and feel for my hoodie and pull it off his face.

Jeepers he is cold.

– Jesus, I say. – Jesus are you dead?

He is just lying there.

I put my head up close to his.

– Jesus are you dead? I say. – Get up.

He doesn't move.

I slap him in the face.

– Get up now and stop this crap, I say.

– Go away Orla, comes a bubbly whisper.

I nod. I thought he was just acting. So I give his face a wipe with the muddy hoody and pull his arm.

– Get up, I say. – You are going to get me all muddy again and last night I was a total disgrace.

– Go away, he says pulling his arm back to him.

So I am not sure what I can do. But I have half an idea so I get up and walk around kicking my feet in front of me and feel something against my toe and it is a goose and I bring it over to where he's lying and get on my knees and open its beak and scrape it against Jesus's wet beard.

– Get off, he says again.

But it works. The goose bucks and thrusts in my hands and bloody hell it freaks me out when it shudders and hisses and I drop it and back off and laugh as it spreads its wings on the mud.

It is the weirdest thing to feel the feathers go from old raggy meat to warm body breathing.

– Why did you do that? says Jesus and now he sits up. He reaches after the goose but his attempt is half-hearted and it just waddles out of his reach.

– Get up, I say. – There is no point lying there like a big idiot.

He rubs his face and doesn't move.

– So get up so.

– You are just a child, he says.

He reminds me of Dad after Mum died.

A fucking wet blanket.

– I am fourteen and a bit, I say. Then, – You have to get up.

– No Orla. You don't understand, he says. – Everything is ruined. Everything.

I kneel down in front of him.

– Yes, I say. – The world is a mess. But you are the Son of God. You have to get up and like covenant everything.

– No!

He actually shouts.

– You do, I say. – You know you have to.

– I am not the Son of God, he says.

Bloody hell.

I'm like, – What do you mean? Look at the goose.

God he is so sorry for himself. I think he is crying in the rain.

Then he's, – If I was the Son of God they would listen to me. I would have the power of tongues and they would hear me and be moved in their hearts. But their hearts are turned from me and I am the sower of gravel in a barren land.

The rain is dying a bit.

I wince as I sit in the mud beside him. My poor clean leggings.

– Come on, I say. – Of course you are the Son of God.

– No! says Jesus. Half a shout again.

At least anger is better than just lying there I guess.

– I am just a half-dead thing. What you said. A husk. I am a husk and I should move into the light of my Father's love.

He sniffs.

– Leave me now, he says. – I am no good to the world.

I sigh. I try to remember anything Sinead said to Dad when he just fucking moped on the sofa for weeks but I never really listened to what they said.

So I go, – Look. Honestly. You have to be the Son of God. And even if you are not the Son of God you are as good as. Who else can like magic things alive again? Who else is going to do it? Those people last night were assholes. Forget about them.

He snuffles a bit and then whispers.

– No Orla, he says. – The Son of God must be for everyone. The Son of God must come not as pointing finger not as fist but as the warm hand.

I just touched him his hands are freezing but I don't say that.

Instead I'm like, – Well okay. Then. I mean if you want to reach them you have to work out how to talk to them. So they will listen. You need what's it called. Showmanship. Razzle dazzle. That's what you need.

Actually yes this works.

He says nothing just keeps snuffling.

I have a little water left in a bottle and I offer it to him. He takes it and drinks. We watch the moor come into view as the clouds part and the big quarter moon carves out the shapes of the dead animals on the grass.

– You lost your bike, I say.

– It was not mine to lose, he says.

– I guess not.

The mud is soaking into my pants again and I cannot be bothered being muddy the whole time so I stand and stretch and walk a bit and then come back. He looks up from the mud.

I'm like, – So come on so. Let's get going.

He doesn't move.

– Come on. Please just come on.

But it's not enough. By the look of him it's going to take more than just talk. So I fix the bags so they don't dangle and reach down and grab his long cold fingers. But honestly it is like that game me and Dad used to play when I'd have to tug him upright from the ground. But I grunt and Jesus lets himself hang until it becomes ridiculous and he has to either pull me down or give up on giving up.

– Come on for Christ's sake just bloody come, I say.

And then he lets himself be pulled. I tug him to his feet and he stumbles and I rebalance him like a drunk at the top of the stairs.

– Can you stand? I say.

– Ngh, he says.

He winces like he is sore.

– I can walk, he says. – But I might need support.

– Good, I say. – We're okay. We'll be okay.

He puts his arm on my shoulder. He is light enough but the wetness and mud make it horrible where he touches me. But his legs work a bit better than last night.

– What about your bike? he says.

It's on its side in the ditch.

– Just leave it, I say. – I'll get it later.

We start walking to the canal. At least the rain has stopped but I know I am going to be all muddy down one side again. But when we get to the water Jesus falls and I have to pick him up.

– Are we going all the way to the boat like this? he says.

– No, I say. – We can't get to Liverpool like this.

He stops walking.

– So how will we get to Ireland?

I don't answer.

– Orla. Where are you taking me?

– The next thing. We're going to the next thing.

He mutters in Bible language. But at least he is moving. But before the mud becomes a path I have another idea and balance him on a fence post. I run back and pick up a dead rabbit and wrap it in my muddy hoody and put it into my bag. Then I run back to Jesus and we lumber on awkwarder than before.

– A bit of razzle dazzle, I say.

43

So when we get to the circus I prop Jesus on the hedge.

    – Wait here, I say.

He nods.

He is still too shivery for much else.

Through the caravans I can see Fantasmo on her knees asleep. Then I pass through the trucks and barrels and washing. There is still one caravan with a light on and a generator humming. I go up to the door and get nervous but I mean what will they do it's not like they can kill me.

Knock knock knock.

There is shuffling inside. I hear a telly. Then a voice.

    – Magda? Is that you? Go to bed.

Silence but for the telly.

    – It's not Magda, I say.

There is more shuffling. Then the door opens a small gap and the face of the ringmaster appears. He is in a dressing gown grizzly and puffy with no makeup. I get a stink of fags and booze from inside.

    – I'm not Magda, I say. – I was at the show tonight.

    – Aye I know you were, he says.

Looks me up and down.

– Fuck off kid, and he closes the door.

I knock again. Try the door.

– No listen I have to talk to you. Open up, I shout.

– Fuck off kid, comes his voice. – You cannae just run off and join the circus.

I knock again.

Hear him turn the volume on the telly up.

He is not doing that to me.

– Help, I shout. – Murder! Rape! Help! A man has got me!

I start shouting and shouting and banging on the door of his caravan. I hear Jesus moving behind me calling, – Orla, and I wave him away to hide. But it works. The old man has shuffled over to pull open the door and the second there is a chink of light I push my whole body in.

He's, – What in the name of fuck are you doing that for?

But I am in.

The caravan is a bright minging disaster. Worse than our house weeks after the funeral. Egg boxes and beer cans and pizza boxes and ashtrays. Laundry mixed with bills and an electric fire and two tellies.

I hear the door close behind me and turn and he whips up a hockey stick and pokes me in the collar bone and says, – You'll not be suing me you wee bastard I am clued in to the likes of you!

And I hold up my hands and even though it would be easy enough to take his stick and bop him in the face with it that is not what I came for so I try the calm-down-Jamie voice.

– Relax relax I am not going to sue you I swear, I say.

His eyes tighten.

With no make-up and hat he is a lot smaller.

– Well if it's money you're after you may keep looking as we have none to give you! And no space for a young girl up the duff looking to run away from her folks.

I blink.

– I'm not. I'm not up the duff, I say.

I don't even look pregnant.

He pokes me in the gut again.

– Well what is it? You want to join the circus like in a movie? Your daddy beating you and your ma's a junkie?

– No! I say.

Feel the anger. Part of me wants to laugh too. Weird.

– No, I say. – I don't want to join. But. But I know an act.

He relaxes and lowers the stick a bit pointing it towards my stomach. Reaches past me for a bottle of beer balanced on a tub of Celebrations. Looks me up and down.

– You're an idiot, he says.

Takes a slug of beer.

– This is not the way to go about these things. This time of night. You could lose a tooth.

He goes to hold out the beer but thinks better of it.

– Girl your age. What do you do? Contortion?

– No. It's not me. I know the act. It's someone else.

I nod and point and awkwardly squeeze past him to the door. Outside there is another caravan with lights on now. The rain has started again light and warm. I go down the steps as the ringmaster stands at his doorway in his dressing gown sipping at his beer jingling his keys.

– Jesus, I call out. – Jesus come here.

I hear the ringmaster chuckle. Across the grass the door of

another caravan opens and the popcorn woman comes out with hair up and she's, – Fucking hell Mickey! But I don't pay her any heed I just call out and Jesus comes limping into the light.

He is a state. More mud than man. Like *The Walking Dead*.

– We don't keep cash here, shouts the woman as she hops back into her caravan pulling her door closed.

The ringmaster makes a gargly sound holding up his stick.

– No, I say. – It's him. He's. He's the act.

And I get down on my knees and take the dead rabbit out of my bag and unwrap it and throw it at Jesus's feet.

Jesus stands there looking down at me.

– What is this Orla?

He doesn't move.

– This is the next thing, I say.

Jesus gives me stink eye like proper raging stink eye like I have never seen before.

– Go on show him, I say. – Show this guy what you can do.

I can hear Jesus breathe and it's not the raggedy breath of a dying man but angry hot breath like a bull.

– You should not test me child, he says.

I shrug.

– Jesus what is the point of a miracle if not to get people to listen to you? You need a bit of showmanship. Razzle dazzle. You could like learn that here. Go on these guys know how to stir up a crowd they are like experts. Just go with them go on and do it for God's sake will you do it? Please do it. Just do it. Do it.

The popcorn woman comes out from her caravan with a kitchen knife and an iPhone and she moves beside the ringmaster. But I keep my eyes on Jesus gangly and suddenly angry and clattered.

– The Son of God is not yours to dispose of Orla. No one is.

And I move up to him whispering fast.

– I know that I can't make you do anything. I know that. But at least get a blanket first a new one a clean one. Ask them if you don't want to lift it. Or maybe stay for a few days ask them for some tricks. Juggling. Razzle dazzle.

He is proper mad.

– What do I know? I say. – I am just a kid.

I can hear the ringmaster muttering but all Jesus has is the raging stink eye.

– Is this why you got us out of bed? says the ringmaster.

I swear I get ten blinks.

– You are a stubborn and very aggravating child, says Jesus.

– Fuck this, says the ringmaster and he unlocks his door.

But then Jesus breaks eye contact with me and kneels down.

He rubs mud off his wrist and bites the skin while his other hand drops to the rabbit. And he lifts the stiff body and kisses it gently on the mouth.

Actually I reckon he probably spits blood into it.

And at first the rabbit hangs from his hand but then twitches and kicks and tries to scratch his wrist and I hear the woman gasp behind me as Jesus puts it down and it doesn't run from the circle of light but just hops a few steps. Nibbles some grass.

The ringmaster comes down the steps and crouches beside the rabbit leaning on his hockey stick.

It doesn't run.

– It's good. I'll give you that, he says. – What is it? Rohypnol? How did you make it so utterly dead looking?

Jesus sighs and lowers his head.

– It is no trick. It is the blood of life.

The ringmaster eyes him.

– What angles does it work from? he says. – The ring is a circle.

Jesus is silent.

– It works on anything dead, I say. – Give him anything. Bats dogs whatever he does them.

– Bollocks it does, says the ringmaster.

But he stays looking at the rabbit.

– You could do that with other animals? says the woman.

Jesus nods.

– Magda get us one of the goldfish. A live one. And why not get a dead one too, says the ringmaster. – In fact bring the lot of them. And a basin. And you big fella what's your name Jesus is it?

He laughs.

– That is my name, says Jesus looking down.

– Well Jesus I am not saying we can take you on. Definitely not in this state or with that name. But let's have a closer look.

He reaches over to pick at the mud caked on Jesus's T-shirt.

– Mister he needs a blanket to sleep under, I say.

But no one is looking at me. The woman comes out with a string of goldfish in plastic bags over her shoulder. Bouncing balls of water each with its own fish. She unspools them into a basin and now the ringmaster is talking low to Jesus.

I can't hear what he is saying.

At first it looks like Jesus is not going to move.

But then Magda gets down beside him and he whispers something to her. She glances at me and whispers something back so I cannot hear it. And then she tilts her head and listens again and nods.

– He likes Wi-Fi, I say. – He likes the internet.

But none of them are listening now. Whatever Jesus said she lets him rest his muddy arm on her shoulder and helps him to his feet. The ringmaster goes to help but Jesus waves him to the basin of bagged fish. He picks them up and follows the pair up the stairs.

Neither Magda nor the ringmaster is looking at me anymore.

Jesus does though. He gives me stink eye over Magda's shoulder the whole way.

I take off his bag and wave it at him and lay it on the grass.

When I look up he is gone.

The ringmaster comes to the door frowning in my direction. The way he stares past my shoulder is like a teacher after the last bell.

– You wait here darling I've only room in there for three.

I shrug as he closes the caravan door behind him.

I mean this suits me perfect.

He's left his keys hanging in the lock.

44

Part of me wants to listen at the door. Hear what they say to Jesus. I mean I feel guilty dumping him. I don't know if he'll stay. Maybe they could like teach him stuff. Maybe.

I mean I hope so.

But also I need a diversion.

So I hold the keys tight so they don't jangle as I slide them from the lock then pick up the old fella's hockey stick from the grass and walk over to the elephant knelt by her cage.

She isn't snoring. I reckon she is awake.

In the little light from the caravan she is bigger than I thought. I know there are different sizes of elephant but not much else. But she is way bigger than any other living thing I have ever touched.

I don't know how to read an elephant's feelings.

Up close she has heavy lashes I mean thick.

But her eye is open. Her black eye.

– Fantasmo, I whisper. – Fantasmo.

I can see where the bandage was on her leg. She has a scabby rough bit on her skin. I touch it very gently with my fingers.

She shifts.

There is a sequiny collar around her neck attached to the lock on the chain. I have to get it off but I have no idea what I am doing. The bunch of keys is massive and the old guy could come out any moment but I reckon he is too interested in Jesus and the fish.

But it will take me ages working through the keys.

I reach in around her massive face.

Her skin rough as dry mud. Her eyes flutter as I get close but she does not panic.

My belly is on her cheek.

– Easy girl, I say.

She probably definitely is a girl.

She shifts when I lean on her and now I can hear her breath. The drizzle has made her damp. I have to put my whole weight on her forehead to get in at her neck. Her trunk lifts and flops onto my shoulders like an arm.

– Easy easy.

I saw the clown put his hand on her nose to stop her moving and tap her knee to get her going. So I rest one palm on her trunk and it feels like a warm tree and I smell the hay of her breath.

– That's it.

I try one key.

It is so awkward.

I nearly drop them but I manage to try a second.

I could be here all night.

But the harness on her neck is just a big double-buckle thing. A belt with two giant straps. I reckon it would be easier to undo the whole thing.

So I nuzzle into Fantasmo and whisper, – Easy easy, like she is a baby waking, – easy easy, careful not to hurt her poor leg slowly climbing onto her back.

The ringmaster is going to come I know it.

So I tug and pull and unclip the first buckle and feel it release.

Then I do the second. I have to pull it harder leaning back with my full weight but I do and it comes undone.

It is a strappy sequin thing. Jammed in the folds in her neck.

– Easy girl. Nearly done now.

I give it a slow yank.

Then the bloody elephant stands up.

First her front legs go. I nearly shout but shut my mouth and clench onto her shoulders with my legs. Then I grab for the hockey stick but it is too late it drops then her back legs go and I grab her ears and now I am high above the ground just hanging on.

I am higher than the caravan.

Fantasmo straightens her neck and steps back and the harness jangles heavily to the ground.

Nobody stirs from the ringmaster's caravan.

I clutch my legs into her rough skin and hold the back of her head. Lying clung full-bodied against her massive leatheriness. My back is cold and wet and she starts moving.

I spot my bag on the grass.

Oh well.

She walks over a fence and I hug like a koala into her shoulders scrunching my face down. I think she could tip me into the canal or just topple and we would both be drowned or she would squash me dead.

My breathing starts to go.

I mean this is all crazy. I am going to fall off. The wheeziness comes then the quick breaths and the harder I clench on the harder it is to breathe. I try sliding lower on her I try the slow counting I go one chihuahua two chihuahua but with every step I jolt and lose the rhythm and I know this is how I am going to die. Runaway orphan dead in freak elephant accident. Bullshit more teen truant dies abusing stolen animal. Dumbo stomps bad bitch. And I deserve it yes I do for dumping Jesus. I deserve it for all I did to Jamie and for abandoning Lily for stealing for hurting Mum Dad too and it is like when Jesus sang I knew I was bad but now it is my fault and yes I am sorry yes but I don't want to die here and I can't breathe the air is too wet I can't breathe.

But then I realise I can feel her breathing.

Catching her breath for a big step.

Each one really slow.

I can feel her breathing against my chest. Through my chest.

I can feel her massive body breathing.

And her breaths are slow and my chest a tiny packet of air but I try to slow my lungs to move with hers.

Slow.

Slow.

I am not saying I learn it but I get more used to the jolt of the back legs the steadier clump of the front and even though I am afraid I get a feel for her pace.

Slow.

It is okay.

I am scared. I am scared.

But it is okay.

It is okay.

Eventually I sit up.

It is dark. The clouds have hunkered down and there is no moon but a warm wind and light drizzle and we are beside a river.

I think the Douglas but it could be the Ribble.

Can elephants see well in the dark?

She seems happy enough to just keep going.

I slide up and wrap my legs around her neck. Shelter them from the drizzle under her ears and hold on to the roots.

Then I bust out laughing.

I mean this is ridiculous. The whole thing is crazy and I must be mad the whole way I have been living is bonkers. But the breeze is lovely and like who cares. Who cares? There is lightning in the distance it could be over the sea or out on the rusty piers at Blackpool I can't be sure which way is which anymore but the sky lights at the edges like there is a war on the other side of the world or a huge fire or some disease that could kill us all. But none of it matters because I have robbed a bloody elephant which is probably the biggest thing anyone has ever robbed in all of Lancashire maybe all the world and I laugh like a big stupid kid.

But there is no one around to tell me I am stupid.

The whole world is mad.

I miss my mum.

She would be so ashamed of me.

Well no that is balls. She would not be ashamed of me. She would shout and tell me that I should not be such a bastard yes she would punish me and we would fight. I know we would. She might laugh later but only later first it would be stop being such a nightmare just be better at home to your dad and at school. Just stop it.

But she'd forgive me.

I know she would.

At some point I lie down to feel the soft roughness of Fantasmo's skin on my whole body and the warmth of her. To feel her breath through her back. I try to move my breath to the rhythm of her breath again. And I don't sleep but I close my eyes for a while. Maybe I half-sleep because sometimes I jerk to keep myself in one place but I try to keep my eyes shut even as I feel the world brightening on my back. I do not know how long it is like that. But eventually I am jerked hard and I open my eyes.

45

Fantasmo is sitting down on all her legs.

We are at a beach.

Well. A wide grassy kind of beach.

I stretch and sit and look about me. It is so bright it hurts my eyes and the sky is the pale before sunrise and there are two muddy streams through the thin grass and the world is incredibly flat. I am all sore from bunching up all night.

Fantasmo grunts.

I think she wants me off.

I want off too.

I climb down and I am all scratchy where my skin was touching her skin but worse busting for a pee and crotchety as heck but I get down beside her and pee and that is a bit better.

She slumps onto her side. Like Sneaky used to do to get you to rub her belly. I don't know if it is the same for elephants but I give her a two-handed scratch.

Seriously those legs could kill me.

But she rolls lying down on her side and I give her another scratch and stare all around. There is like nothing for miles.

No houses. No wait. Over there is the sea but closer this way I can see two cars. Maybe a road?

My best guess is we are somewhere on the Ribble where it stretches to the sea. But I have no real idea.

No idea what time it is either but mist is rising off the ground.

I sigh.

No food no clothes. No bag. No bike.

I am hungry and tired. And Fantasmo seems done walking.

So I give her one last scratch and start walking towards the cars and the road. I think I can see two people up there.

Dog walkers I reckon.

I can see their dogs. Two of them. No four. Four dogs.

Women. One in a blue anorak and one in suede.

Older than my dad.

– Alright hen? says one when they get close.

– What are you doing out here? says the other.

I ask them where the road leads. Hesketh Bank.

– What's your name hen?

– Nothing, I say. – My name is nothing.

It is a stupid answer.

– What is your name darling? Everyone's got a name there's no harm in it we are not out to get you.

– Have you run away from home pet? Tell us sweetheart we won't hurt you. You can come with us.

– My name is Sophie. Sophie Jenkins, I say.

But it is too late they don't believe me. But I refuse to come and say my dad is picking me up at Hesketh we were camping but they don't believe anything I say now probably because of the state of my clothes or maybe because I can't be arsed telling it right. But they are kind and give me a banana which I eat there and then and also a packet of Extra which I save. But they don't like me throwing the banana peel on the ground and one of them picks it up and the other one holds my arm and gets her phone out.

Who the fuck is she gonna call social services?

I am not ready for that. Not yet.

– Is that an elephant? I say.

Over in the mist the dogs have found Fantasmo. Maybe she has found them I am not sure. But she is chasing them and I burst out laughing as the mist clears and in the distance you can hear the yipping of dogs as Fantasmo trots after them.

I can feel her footsteps through my feet.

Maybe she is just playing but who knows what goes on in an elephant's mind maybe she always hated the circus dog and is out for revenge lol. All I can see is the dogs running against a blue sky and the elephant pounding after like a holy terror.

The women see it and start shouting.

– Nigel! Nigel! shouts one as they run in the direction of the dogs.

I guess she called her dog Nigel.

They leave me alone laughing and I watch for a second because I'd love to see what the women plan to do to stop an elephant chasing their dogs but instead I head down towards the road. I know the women might cause trouble later with their phones but I reckon right now all they are thinking about is Fantasmo and poor Nigel.

46

I mean I am working on borrowed time now. It was stupid to phone Sinead. But I am not sure I care anymore.

I keep thinking about tea and toast.

I remember when I was tiny Mum used to make me milky tea and I would dip buttered toast in and it would go horrible and sloppy but when I sucked the bread it filled my mouth with this warm buttery sweetness.

I can't get it out of my head.

I could really do with that.

All I have is this gum.

And thirty-odd quid in the bumbag.

But the world is so cool and bright it hurts my eyes and I chew through the gum but it doesn't make me less thirsty.

When I get to the road I am a bit scared of seeing real day people again but I need something. To eat or drink.

I see a bus and it is going left.

I reckon wherever the bus is going there will be food.

There are houses here now but further down the road there are more as the countryside turns into village.

I pass a woman pushing a buggy and I reckon I look like a

girl out of a horror movie. There are big brown marks on my side and on my leggings. But it's alright she barely looks up from her phone.

I pass a pharmacy.

All they ever have is cough sweets.

So I keep walking.

There are more houses and then I am on a real street and then I come to a Co-op. I drag my fingers through my hair but it is hopeless. So I just go in head down.

Fanta. Packet of baby tomatoes. Tangy cheese Doritos.

– Just these thanks.

Costs £3.25.

I have to break a tenner but I needn't have worried the woman barely sees me.

So I sit in their crappy roadside car park and start the Doritos and they are rank but full of lovely salt and I wash them down with Fanta. It's too sweet. A poor excuse from toast dipped in tea. I try a baby tomato to make me feel better but then I see a white Toyota across from me.

We have a white Toyota.

It takes me like a minute.

But that's our car.

When I realise it I spill Fanta slowly down my arm.

I walk up to it.

He is there in the front seat.

I think he's asleep.

Slowly I put down the Fanta and look in the windows.

It's Dad.

Open-mouthed head back snoring in the front seat.

Lily is in the back. Asleep as well.

I wonder if they have slept in this crappy car park all night or did they stop here when the sun came up and why is Lily with him and not with Sue?

I lick the Fanta off my wrist.

There is no way he would know if I just legged it.

I could catch a bus.

Now. Just go.

Anywhere in the world.

I don't want to go anywhere.

I want toast and tea.

So slowly very slowly I get in the front seat.

Neither of them moves.

After a while I cough.

Nothing.

With one finger I poke him very gently on the cheek.

I watch as he opens his eyes.

Closes them.

Then he jumps.

– Fuck!

He flails about like he is drowning and then says, – Fuck! again and grabs my arm and says, – Fuck, once more and then opens his door and walks off up the road leaving me and Lily in the car.

I run out and he is already halfway down the street.

– Dad!

How can he just leave Lily like that?

– Dad!

He turns.

– A fucking knife?

He is shouting. An old woman tuts at him across the street.

– You fuck off and all, he says.

Bloody hell he must be bad he has not cursed at randomers since the church. His arms are everywhere and his face is raggedy and pink.

– What are you on about?

– A fucking knife. I have been talking with the cops and they said they are looking for a girl of your description who stabbed a fucking woman in a pub just down the road from here?

Ah.

Stabbed!

– She had a tiny cut on her finger! I say. – And she was grabbing me and wouldn't let go and a fella was being battered what do you expect me to do let him die? There were like two bouncers smashing his face up!

And he's up at me and he's saying, – Shhhh! but really loudly spitting at his finger and trying to whisper and his face is wreckage.

– Do you have any idea how much bother you will be in if they can pin this on you? It's not ha ha like dobbing fucking Science! It's locked up forever with the proper bad bastards! And I am trying everything I mean everything to keep you living with me and Lily and they are that close to taking you away that fucking close and if they pin this on you you are toast!

Toast.

Toast and tea.

And I try not to I know it is the wrong time but trying not to makes it worse and I bust out laughing.

He stares at me.

His head shudders and he blinks but I can't stop laughing.

– Bastard! he shouts pointing at me.

And he walks off.

He stomps past me and gets to the car before I do because the laughing slows me but when I get to him he has opened the boot. And he has a rucksack in his hand a big one like for camping not for school and he fires it at the kerb before me.

– You want to go to live with Sinead? Aye she phoned me and all. Well on you go so on you fucking go. There's the rest of your clothes.

And he gets in the car.

And sits there.

I mean he is bluffing.

But when I jiggle the handle he has it locked and I stop grinning.

– Open the fucking door.

I mean I am so tired it has been so many days I have no patience for his bullshit. God I need a shower it would be great. But then he turns the ignition.

He is bluffing and I cannot be bothered so I hit the window.

– Open up!

Then he drives off.

– Dad!

I run after him a bit but I am too tired and I stop.

But he turns the corner.

And I don't know what to do so I scream. Long and hard as I used to when I was a kid I can feel it in my eardrums like a rip in my neck and this is not fair and the woman from the Co-op is out touching my arm and I pull away from her in the middle of the road just screaming and there are like three other people in the door of the Co-op and then my dad reverses around the corner beside me and winds down his window.

– What? he says.

I catch my breath.

– What?

– I want to come home, I say.

He doesn't move.

His hand still on his keys.

– I'll go see Claire, I say.

His eyes all bloodshot and wrinkles. But he takes his hand off the keys and opens his door and for a second I think he is going to smack me in the face but he grabs me and pulls me into his jacket.

– Don't ever fucking do that to me again pet I cannot take it.

I let him hug me for a couple of seconds.

It's alright.

Then he picks up the rucksack of clothes and puts it in the boot and I could get in the front but I don't I get in beside Lily who is asleep scrunching her face and I touch her cheek and she opens her eyes and blinks twice.